That had been close. Too close.

No suspect was worth what had almost happened. Kendall had to be more careful, less reckless. Skylar Dawn needed her parents to come home.

"You okay?" Heath asked, back at the passenger door. She nodded, still a little stunned by it all.

"I can't say I'm bummed about them getting away." The corner of his mouth barely rose as he leaned on the car.

"What? Why's that?"

"Where's the fun in catching them the first day I get to work with you again?" He said it with such a straight face that if she hadn't known him she never would've seen that playful gleam in his eye.

She couldn't argue with that logic either. She would've been bummed, too.

RANGER GUARDIAN

USA TODAY Bestselling Author

ANGI MORGAN

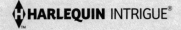

Thank you, Amanda! Thanks for the encouragement and the major kick in the behind—just the right amount of both. And a special thanks for being such a great person to model a character after!

ISBN-13: 978-1-335-52650-2

Ranger Guardian

Copyright © 2018 by Angela Platt

Recycling programs for this product may not exist in your area.

Printed in U.S.A.

HARLEQUIN®
www.Harlequin.com

Angi Morgan writes about Texans in Texas. A *USA TODAY* and *Publishers Weekly* bestselling author, her books have been finalists for several awards, including the Booksellers' Best Award, *RT Book Reviews* Best Intrigue Series and the Daphne du Maurier. Angi and her husband live in North Texas. They foster Labradors and love to travel, snap pics and fix up their house. Hang out with her on Facebook at Angi Morgan Books. She loves to hear from fans at angimorganauthor.com.

Books by Angi Morgan

Harlequin Intrigue

Visit the Author Profile page at Harlequin.com.

CAST OF CHARACTERS

Heath Murray—A Texas Ranger who wants to guard his wife and daughter at all costs. He lives on a ranch with his Company B partner just outside Dallas.

Kendall Barlow—FBI agent, mom, wife, daughter... Can she be everything or does she need to choose one?

Skylar Dawn Barlow Murray—The almost four-year-old freckle-faced daughter of Heath and Kendall. She's just beginning to love riding ponies.

Public Exposure—Headed by Brantley Lourdes. On the surface it's an organization that wants kids and adults to give up social media. But does it have a hidden agenda?

Slate Thompson—Lieutenant in the Texas Rangers and Heath's roommate and partner in Company B.

Wade Hamilton—Lieutenant in the Texas Rangers, Company B. He has a habit of acting before he thinks things through and always trusts his gut.

Jack MacKinnon, Jr.—Lieutenant in the Texas Rangers, Company B, and Heath's coworker.

Jerry Fisher—FBI special agent in charge, Dallas. Kendall's former partner and now her supervisor.

Naomi Barlow—Kendall's mother, who has never approved of Heath.

Therese Ortis—A mysterious woman associated with an unknown organization. Who she really is is the question of the day. Wade owes her a favor.

Prologue

Eight Months Ago

Heath Murray rushed through the emergency room doors. Yes, he'd used the entrance for the ambulances. Yes, he'd parked his truck next to the building, practically on the sidewalk. And yes, he'd taken advantage of having the Texas Ranger badge he carried.

What did anyone expect? His three-year-old daughter was there. It was the only thing he knew for sure. The message from his wife had stated only what hospital they were heading to.

Life was good. Life was perfect. He couldn't imagine life without his baby girl, Skylar Dawn, in it. He couldn't imagine life without his wife, Kendall. Six years ago, if you'd asked him if his life would be full of anything except law enforcement, he would have answered no.

Now?

Life was full of pink frills and satin sun dresses. Along with brand new ponies—plastic and real. And all the disagreements about whether Skylar Dawn was old enough to own a pony. Yep, life was full, and he was blessed several times over.

He rushed to his mother-in-law, who stood up from a waiting room chair. Her eyes were red but not swollen. Her old-fashioned handkerchief was twisted and streaked from her mascara. She looked like she'd been pulled straight out of a church service, but Naomi Barlow looked like that every day. And she didn't go to church.

"Where is she?"

"Kendall is with her. She's going to be fine. It's not a break that will require surgery."

"What kind of an accident were they in?"

"Accident? Did you think they were in a car accident?" Kendall's mom asked, then laughed.

What the hell? Why was she laughing?

"Where are they?"

"Oh, honey, you poor thing. Skylar Dawn just fell on the playground at day care. That's all. She'll be fine." Naomi's eyes darted toward a set of double doors. "Only one person can be in the room with her."

He didn't need her response. What he did need was for the attendant to open the doors from the other side.

"Excuse me." He headed straight to the front desk and flipped his badge so the person at the window could see it. "I need to get through."

"May I see your credentials?"

Heath shot his ID through the slot and managed to keep his toes from tapping the linoleum while he waited. "Thanks," he added politely to the man whose turn he'd interrupted, then paced back to his mother-in-law and handed her his keys. "Give these to the green-faced Texas Ranger who comes inside in a minute. My partner, Slate Thompson will take my truck home."

"Here you go, sir. I can buzz you through now."

He heard the door lock open and hurried to pull on the handle, but it opened at a snail's pace on its own. He rushed down the hall, glancing through the small windows. Then he heard her.

A quiet, polite cry for a child of three.

He rounded a corner and took a deep breath. *Okay, they really are all right.* He hadn't processed that information when Naomi had told him. He couldn't believe it until he'd seen with his own eyes.

So he took a second. They'd be upset as it was. He didn't need to add to the situation by not appearing calm. He shook his shoulders, slowed his racing pulse, became the dad instead of the Ranger who'd driven ninety across Dallas to get here.

"There they are." He thought his voice sounded excited to see them, instead of like the frightened-to-death man who'd just had his heart ripped from his chest.

"See, I told you Daddy was on his way."

"Daddy!" Skylar Dawn tried to lift her free arm to him. "I want Daddy."

"It's better if you stay where you are, baby. Mommy's got you." He honestly didn't think his shaking arms could hold her steadily.

Kendall tilted her cheek up for a kiss. He rubbed Skylar Dawn's strawberry blond hair. One day it would be as thick as her mother's and out of the small pigtails.

"How 'bout I sit down here so you can see me?" He sat on the floor, pulling himself close to his wife and daughter, just about ready to cry from the gratitude he felt at them both being alive and safe.

There was no tension in Kendall. She seemed far

calmer than her message had implied. She mouthed, "Sorry."

His wife could probably tell how frantic he was. She'd always been good at picking up on the nuances that gave away his emotions. In fact, she was practically the only person who had ever been able to see through the wall he'd built.

A wall that had been breached several times over by Skylar Dawn.

"Let me see." He leaned closer and puckered his lips for a loud smack without ever touching the skin of her arm. "Does that feel better?"

Skylar Dawn shook her head. "I broke it, Daddy. Does that mean we have to throw it away?"

He refrained from chuckling. "No, baby girl. The doctors can fix this all up. And you'll be as good as new."

"Oh, that's a relief." She perfectly imitated her mother.

"I've been explaining that her arm isn't a toy." Kendall smiled.

"No throwaway arms," he said.

Skylar Dawn dropped her head to Kendall's chest. "Just close your eyes for a minute, sweetheart," said Kendall. "I'll wake you up when the doctor comes back."

He placed a hand on Skylar Dawn's back and could feel when her body relaxed into sleep. *Nice to be a kid.*

"What took you so long?" Kendall whispered.

He followed suit, whispering back his answer. "We were in west Fort Worth. I did ninety most of the way. Slate thought he was going to puke."

"I just… I'm sorry about the wild message. The day care called without a lot of details. Then they told me I couldn't use my cell phone back here. I should have had Mother call with an update. I know it scared you."

"I'm good. All's good."

He listened to the details of Skylar Dawn climbing the section of the playground her age group wasn't allowed on. One of the older girls—probably about five—had helped her. Skylar Dawn had fallen.

They whispered about the X-ray and doctor's analysis. Just a hairline fracture, but they could go to the pediatrician for a cast in a couple of days.

The love Kendall had for their daughter radiated like sunshine. How awesome would it be to have another little girl as precious as this one?

The doctor came and went. Heath took Skylar Dawn from Kendall's arms and cuddled her against his chest. Her head had a special baby smell that he especially noticed when she first fell asleep. It was something he already knew he'd miss whenever she got too big to be rocked.

"Hey, for a couple who never wanted children, I think we're handling this pretty well." Kendall smoothed Skylar Dawn's hair while they waited on their release paperwork.

"Want to have a couple more?" he said, then gulped.

"What?" Kendall's eyes grew big. "Where does this come from?"

"It was just a thought. I mean…I love you guys. I love our family. And you're right. I think we're pretty good at this."

"I do, too."

Were those tears?

"Honey, what's wrong?" He opened his free arm and pulled her in for a hug.

Special Agent Kendall Barlow was full-blown crying, silent tears running down her face. And it took a lot—like the birth of their daughter—to bring them on. Heath never expected his spontaneous suggestion to affect her this way.

"I was… I was…" she tried.

"It's okay, babe. Everything's perfect the way it is. Nothing's wrong with our family."

"But I was just thinking the same thing, Heath. I'd love another baby."

He kissed her. As much as he was able to with his arms full of their daughter.

"I am definitely looking forward to getting you home and getting this one in bed." He waggled his eyebrows at her.

Kendall dabbed at her eyes. "We can't start this afternoon, silly. I'm helping Jerry with his cyber-fraud case. It's going to take weeks. Maybe months."

"You want to wait?" He was surprised. Seriously surprised. And then an ugly voice shouted in his ear, *How many cases will be more important?*

"Whisper, please?"

"Sure." He lowered his voice to match hers. "Why would finishing cases be more important? It's not like you'll still be trying to move up the FBI ladder."

"I beg your pardon?"

"Well, if you have another baby, aren't you quitting?"

The words were there before he could mentally slap

himself and stop them from forming. Mistake. It was the wrong thought to let out of his mouth.

"You want me to quit my job and stay home? What? Do you want me barefoot and pregnant in the kitchen, too?"

He tucked his bottom lip between his teeth. He wasn't going to say a word. Not a dad-blasted word. It wasn't the time. It wasn't the place.

Then she stiffened and pulled away from his arm. *Dammit.*

"Kendall, we thought having any kids in day care whose parents are both in the line of fire wasn't a good idea. It's still not a good idea. But two? If you're pregnant, they'll call you out of the field anyway. Right?"

"For a few months. Just like last time. But I'm not going to give up my career. You stay home with the kids."

"I worked hard to be a Texas Ranger."

"And I worked hard to become an FBI agent."

It was the loudest whispered arguing they'd ever done. It gave him a bad feeling, like something ominous was about to happen.

"Maybe we should talk about this at home." He kissed his daughter's forehead. "When the munchkin is in bed, we can list the pros and cons."

"Or we could be honest with each other."

"I think I've been honest enough."

"Oh, that's a relief." She crossed her arms in typical Barlow fashion, after her sarcasm had a chance to sink in.

"It's going to be a long night, isn't it," he said. Fact, not a question. Just like he knew they were stepping outside into the backyard to have an extended argument once they got home.

"We both need to really think about your expectations for me. This is serious, Heath. I… It's not something I can take lightly and just forget that it happened."

"I'm sorry for jumping the gun." Apologizing was the easy part. Understanding what he did wrong would take a little longer.

SIX WEEKS OF continuous arguing began to take its toll on her family. Kendall sat at her office desk staring at the picture of Heath carrying Skylar Dawn on his shoulders. She missed him. Ached for him. Longed for someone to invent a time machine so she could take back the words she didn't even know if she meant any more. Just when Kendall thought things were getting better, her mother overheard Heath say he didn't understand why her work was more important than a family.

She didn't know which hurt worse—what he'd said or the fact he had talked to someone else and not her. He'd always been the strong silent type. Definitely a man of action and few words.

When Skylar Dawn complained of tummy aches, Kendall suggested counseling. If they couldn't communicate on their own, maybe a third party could help.

She'd never forget the stabbing pain she'd experienced when he said, "My world has pretty much crashed down around my ears by not keeping my mouth shut." To keep from hurting their daughter, Heath packed a bag. He made a drastic, solitary decision.

If he was gone…they couldn't argue. So to solve the problem he moved into the spare room of Slate Thompson's house on a small ranch just east of Dallas. He worked in the barn and helped with riding lessons to pay his rent.

Or at least that's what she thought. They hadn't really spoken since.

They seemed to avoid each other by staying busy with their jobs. But he never failed to call Skylar Dawn at six each evening. When her caseload picked up, he stayed at the house two nights a week.

Her mother had objected to her marriage from the beginning. For some reason, her encouragement had always been for a career. Not necessarily the FBI, just something with a title and advancement.

"How did we get this far down the rabbit hole? Yeah… Where's that time machine when you need it?"

Chapter One

Heath Murray was feeling just how crowded the small house he lived in had become. He slipped away to the rodeo every weekend, attempting to give Slate some privacy. But, man, come Sunday nights he needed to rest his weary old bones on a soft couch.

He needed to pop the top on a bottle of beer, prop his feet up on the coffee table and listen to sports while he drifted off into blissful slumber.

That never happened.

He didn't mind having his partner's mom cook. Saved him the trouble of constantly eating out. He didn't mind having Slate's new girlfriend sneak back up to the main house after not catching the front door before it slammed shut at four in the morning. Neither of them knew he hadn't really slept in months.

He didn't mind returning to his real bed twice a week to spend time with his baby girl. Skylar Dawn loved it. Kendall tolerated it. They both agreed it was better than the nights he didn't see their daughter at all.

He could deal with all that. He'd been dealing with it for almost six months. But this...

"Dammit, guys. Do you always have to be making out when I open the door?"

"Oh, man. Is it already five? I'm supposed to go see my brother tonight. I should go get ready." Vivian Watts, his roommate's girlfriend, tugged her T-shirt to her waist, making sure it was in place. She gave Slate a quick kiss and ran past Heath.

"Thanks for making her feel bad," Slate said.

"Don't mention it." Yeah, he was being sarcastic. Yeah, he didn't mean to be. Hell, maybe he did. His attitude sucked, and his side hurt. The bronc he'd been thrown from had kicked his ribs. The skin had begun turning colors before he'd started for home.

"Well, I sort of am." Slate took his hands from his back pockets and crossed his arms in a move of determination. "You know she's had a really hard time lately. They told her it's going to be at least another six weeks before they'll think about clearing her brother to leave the center."

"Sorry. I didn't mean it and I'll apologize." He would. He'd probably screw up again, though. "Maybe it's time for me to find my own place?"

"That's not what you need to do," Slate said with a certain look on his face.

The same frustrated look his friends and fellow Rangers had at least once a week. Maybe even a little more often. Like each time they tried to get him to open up about his situation with his wife. Yet if he couldn't talk about it with her, he shouldn't talk about it with his friends. Their separation was a private matter.

"You, me, Wade and Jack are tight. We're more than just Rangers, and we're more than friends. We're brothers.

We've got each other's backs. I'm telling you the truth. You should call her," Slate urged.

"I will. Tuesday."

"You are such a stubborn son of a...cowboy."

At that, Heath tipped his hat off his head and let the Stetson flip into his hand. A trick his little girl loved.

"You better head on out if you're going to catch Vivian and drive her to her brother's."

"Call your wife, man. Make up. It's been six months, for crying out loud. Tell her you don't think your job is more important than hers."

"You don't think I've told her? I haven't ever lied to her. I thought she knew that. But for some reason she still can't believe me." He pulled a beer from the refrigerator, glancing at the plastic containers full of home-cooked meals. He was too sore to eat.

"Dammit, Heath." Slate stuck a ball cap on his head. "Think hard about what you're willing to give up." He stomped to the door and slammed it shut behind him.

Alone.

It was how he liked it. Right?

"Right," he spoke out loud and tipped the beer he'd wanted for the past hour between his lips and swallowed.

Another couple of minutes, and he could call Skylar Dawn before Kendall put her in the bathtub. She was almost four years old, and it had been six months since he'd destroyed any chance at a normal father-daughter relationship.

He went through the motions, just like he did every night. Nothing there comforted him like it had when he was married. There was no one to talk to about the bronc ramming him in half.

No one to joke with about the young women hanging around the edge of the stalls. Or how he'd felt too old to notice. But they'd had fun with their wolf calls when he'd bent over and showed his backside. Kendall had gotten a kick out of coming up and laying a big, luscious kiss on him when that had happened before.

That had been before she'd gotten pregnant and the barn smell had made her nauseous.

Another sip of beer. It was almost gone, and he wanted another.

Was this what life was going to be like? Waiting around while Kendall—and her mother—made all the decisions about their life? He'd been ready for months to talk with her and apologize again. He just wanted their old life back.

Was that even possible?

Completely aware that pressure against his side would be painful, he went back into the kitchen, filled a couple of sandwich bags with ice, wrapped them in a towel and shoved it against his ribs.

The stinging cold brought him to his senses. He was getting too old for this routine. Too old to be afraid to talk with his wife. Too old to insult Vivian and Slate or any of his other friends because he was miserable with his own life.

It was time to make some changes.

Good or bad…he needed to talk with Kendall face-to-face. Soon. Maybe it would turn out better than he feared. Maybe it wouldn't. All he knew was that it was time to move forward.

Good thing he had a light load at work. He was mostly focused on court and testifying and paperwork right now. He set the ice on the table, then slid his shirt free from his belt. He tucked it up close to his armpit before looking closer at the bruise.

That was going to be a big boo-boo, as baby girl would say.

Yeah, it was time. Slate was right about that. Time to apologize and move on. How long could a woman stay mad?

Something in the back of his mind warned that *his* woman could stay that way a very, very long time. Especially with a mother whispering in her ear who hated him. Hell, his mother-in-law had shouted to the world that he'd never be good enough for her daughter.

He clicked on his phone, stared at the picture of Kendall holding a super pink baby girl and swiped to dial. He would talk to his wife face-to-face. Tonight, he'd read to his daughter.

"Hey there. How's my favorite munchkin?" He reached for the children's version of *The Wizard of Oz*.

"Daddy!"

"Jerry, I know it's Sunday night. That's why I'm calling. I need more people. I know I'm close to a breakthrough." Kendall Barlow didn't back down. Her supervisory special agent should know that. She heard the house phone ring in the background, as it did every night like clockwork.

In six months' time, Heath hadn't missed calling his daughter once. And not one time had he made a serious effort to reconcile. He was a man of few words—for everyone except Skylar Dawn.

"Kendall. It's been months and you've got nothing to show for it. You know we're shorthanded. Dallas Police Department is worse off than we are. You aren't going to get more qualified personnel for the joint task force than the people already assigned to it."

"If I had another competent person who knew their way around computers, I know I could prove that Public Exposure is fraudulent. We're close. Very close."

"Oh furgle. Our resources have been tapped out. Run with what you've got, and get me something to show for your time. Of course, there is one person already on your task force you haven't tried."

"Special Agent Fisher, I've asked you not to use that word. I've looked it up and it's inappropriate. It was fine in *Catch-22*, but come on. You know it doesn't mean what you think." She was tired of this conversation. Or was he trying to distract her? Did he really think that she needed something to justify the investigation? Couldn't he think of one more possible agency to check? "Jerry?"

"Yes? I promise I'll behave. I just love that word."

"Please don't—"

"You should talk to your ex. Ask him if he's heard anything about your case."

"That's a clear conflict of interest. No one would allow him on the team."

"Seems like that's my decision now. I'll allow him to help out until the Rangers can find a replacement. Use the taxpayers' money wisely. See you in the office."

The line disconnected, and she could once again

hear the exclamations of surprise from her daughter as her father read about flying monkeys and sparkly red shoes. Had she mentioned to Heath that their daughter had outgrown two pairs of those red slippers while he'd been gone?

Skylar Dawn was sitting on the couch holding the main phone extension. Her grandmother listened on an additional handset just outside the door. Heath knew about the eavesdropping even if her mother thought it was a secret. He accepted it as part of his "punishment for whatever he blamed himself."

As if living away from their precious little girl wasn't punishment enough. Why he thought he needed to be punished, she didn't understand. And no matter how she tried, her mother wouldn't stop.

Constant jabs at Heath kept an undercurrent of tension in the air. Kendall wanted to avoid the subject and leaned toward avoiding her mother in the evenings when she helped out with Skylar Dawn.

Heath wasn't her ex, and finalizing their separation wasn't high on her priority list. So far there hadn't been any squabbles about how to do anything. He'd taken only a few of his things and the horses.

Other than a picture or two of Skylar Dawn, he'd managed to leave everything looking exactly like it had been when he'd walked away. Or when she'd driven him away. She could remember exactly when things had come to a pivotal breaking point. Most of that argument had to do with her mother.

Her mother's standards had been high her entire life. Heath had a father exactly the same way. But what had turned Heath into a strong man who held his opinions to himself—or himself and his horse—seemed to be turning her soul bitter.

I can't be my mother. I can't do that to Skylar Dawn.

"Do you have to say goodbye, Daddy?"

Kendall waited for the familiar "Good night" and "I love you." Her daughter clicked the red button on the phone and her mother followed a second afterward. She crossed her arms, enveloping the phone between a breast and a well-toned limb.

Her mother, a woman of sixty, made good use of the money she'd gathered over the years. Three step-fathers and three settlements later, Kendall had a college education and two letters of recommendation for her Bureau interview.

Getting along with the men in her mother's life had never been the problem. More and more recently, she'd been realizing how sad her mother had become. And how demanding.

Her mother didn't allow Skylar Dawn two seconds to linger or even to put the phone back on its charging station. She immediately clapped her hands, and her granddaughter jumped to her feet.

Oh my God! She's reacting like a trained puppy.

Kendall swooped in and picked up her little girl, who should need a bath from playing in the dirt. But she was perfectly clean.

"Wow. Let's go for a ride. What do you think, sweet girl?"

"Kendall, I was just getting ready to run her bath. Isn't it late to go out?"

"Actually, Mother, you might be right. But we're going anyway." Kendall smiled and steadied her daughter back down on her feet. "Let's go see if we can find some flying monkeys."

Skylar Dawn giggled as they skipped down the hall and out the front door.

It was clear that changes needed to be made for her and her daughter. She'd set paperwork in motion the next day. She'd find out the possibilities before she approached Heath.

Six months of living with her mother instead of her husband was long enough. Five minutes down the road, she realized she'd pointed the car east toward Heath. She slowed and turned into a drive-through. Then they got ice cream and played at the park until they both really needed a bath.

It was fun. Spontaneous. She used to be those things. It was the whole reason Skylar Dawn had come to be.

It was time to find that person again.

Chapter Two

Wade Hamilton shoved the last file into the back of the box. It represented months of work and the official end of his desk duty. It had taken him almost as long to heal from the beating he'd received six months ago. But everything worked again. Both with his body and his status as a Texas Ranger Company B lieutenant.

Ready to take his place at his partner's side. Ready to get out from behind his desk. Back to handling things by the seat of his pants instead of the rule book. Doing so had landed him in this desk chair. He'd learned his lesson to slow down and think a little. He liked field-work…not paperwork.

Unfortunately, Major Clements had discovered Wade was good at paper shuffling. He'd been allowed to assist with a few cases as backup for Company B brothers. But the paperwork grew while he was gone.

It seemed like the rest of the office had grown accustomed to him shuffling their requests, too. Coming in early and staying late was second nature now. Why not, since he had no life?

That's where he was bright and early on a Monday morning. At work before the rest of the staff or other

Rangers finished their first cup of coffee, he was shuffling papers. Almost done, the latest request for his company's support caught his eye. He knew the name of the FBI agent heading the task force. He'd attended her wedding just over five years ago.

Kendall Barlow was the new team leader of a cyber-crime task force and asking for computer and field support on the joint task force. Heath—her husband and the logical choice—had already been assigned to cybercrime. Now their relationship would need to be reviewed and disclosed. He'd been on the task force since it was headed by Jerry Fisher. But still, Murray was the best geek Company B had.

It was up to Wade to recommend someone else or okay Heath for a couple of days in the field with Special Agent Barlow.

It was also an opportunity to resolve his friend's problem. He'd been listening to Slate talk about his temporary roommate for six months. How he worked the horses, cleaned the stalls, never missed a phone call with his daughter and never—ever—spoke to his wife. Heath, on the other hand, never said a word. Wade held on to the paperwork and grabbed a second cup of coffee.

Who was he to jump in to the middle of a man's business? Especially marriage problems? But the more he tried to talk himself out of it, the more his gut told him to assign Heath to work with his wife.

Slate and Jack were both standing at his desk when he returned from the break room. Before he asked their advice, Jack pointed to the request.

"What's this?"

"You're sending him, right?" Slate asked. "It's exactly what they both need to force them to figure out what's going on."

"You think so?"

"Damn straight," they answered together.

"The man's turning into a bear," Slate said. "I might take his head off if he snarls at Vivian again."

"If the FBI put in the request, you should accommodate it," Jack stated, hanging his jacket on the rack.

"What if *she* doesn't want it?" Wade asked, already knowing that he would recommend Heath.

"Then she has a friend who is thinking along the same lines we are." Slate took his seat opposite Wade. "Maybe she's as cranky as he is."

"Who's cranky?" Heath asked as he walked through the door.

"The old man, Major Clements," Jack said, jumping in. "We're coming up with reasons he might be out of sorts. I say he's getting ready to retire. Wade says his wife might be cranky."

"My bet's on the wife." Heath winced as he took off his jacket, holding his side. "The old man's never going to retire."

The guys nodded in agreement. Slate mouthed "Bear," while pointing to Heath behind his hand.

Wade recognized Heath's movement. When his own ribs had been cracked, he'd held his side the same way. Heath had probably injured himself at the rodeo this weekend. But he'd never admit it.

Wade agreed with hiding it from the boss. If he hadn't been unconscious with an eye swollen twice its size, he probably would have taken a couple of days off and never admitted anything about the beating. Or about the woman who'd saved his life by alerting Jack to his whereabouts.

Time to put his own fantasies to rest and find the woman who haunted his dreams… Therese. If he couldn't work on that, the least he could do was help get Heath and Kendall back together.

He reached for the request, ready to recommend his friend and submit it to Major Clements. The old man would make the final decision if Company B would waive the conflict of interest. Maybe Heath and Kendall could find mutual ground and resolve their differences.

If not, then this assignment would at least help them reach that decision, too.

He completed the paperwork and sent it on its way. Assignment made.

Chapter Three

Heath held his side as he carefully lifted his arm into his suit jacket and then set his white Stetson on top of his head. The required Texas Ranger uniform wasn't what people expected when they saw the star on his pocket. Traditionally they all wore white Stetsons, but with suits rather than jeans. He even wore a white shirt and black tie today.

Good thing, since he'd been assigned to work with an FBI task force regarding potential cybercrime. The agent in charge thought a research company had some type of ulterior motive for collecting the data.

Cybercrime had a broad definition—it referred to any crime committed with a computer or through a computing device. The slim file he'd received held just the basics and an address where to meet the agent. He was curious to learn what had tipped the FBI off and what the specifics of the case were.

Why meet here in the field? It wasn't the norm. Neither was getting a last-minute request for field backup on a task force he hadn't been active with for a while. Jerry Fisher—his wife's old partner—had been promoted to group leader overseeing several teams in cybercrime. What was different now?

He waited for this mysterious agent at his truck. The older neighborhood was nicely kept up. The homes were on the smaller side for this section of Dallas. They'd eventually be sold and torn down to make way for larger lots.

It was a shame. Some of them looked really nice and were perfect starter places for couples. *Or to house mothers-in-law.* He'd been thinking about his wife the entire trip across town.

Only natural that he'd start thinking of her mother, since he half blamed her for egging on their arguments. He'd gone back and forth long into the night about calling Kendall. Even picked up his phone a couple of times. But the chicken part of himself won.

What if that phone call ended everything?

This morning he watched the sun rise while riding his mare and resolved to call Kendall today to make a date to talk. Not over the phone. Not around Skylar Dawn. Certainly not around his mother-in-law. The promise gave him peace of mind. Six months was enough time apart. He needed to try again. Speaking face-to-face would allow him to gauge her reaction. And if she called it quits?

Well, he wanted her to look him in the eye if she did.

There were several cars on the street of the address he'd been given. None of them were a government-issued sedan. He glanced at his watch—only a couple of minutes early.

If he was working with the FBI, he'd eventually have to visit their Dallas field office. He wasn't excited about running into Kendall accidentally. Or her supervisor, Jerry Fisher.

Whoever his partner from the FBI was, they were late. Unless he was supposed to meet them inside. He walked around the truck, calling Wade to see if there'd been a time adjustment to the appointment. When a black sedan pulled up behind his truck, he disconnected. He leaned on the tailgate while putting his phone away, waiting.

"Heath?" A familiar voice rang from the far side of the government car.

The car door shut, and he stood at attention for some reason. The face came into focus while his body charged out of control.

Kendall?

Dammit. He'd almost dove into the truck bed. Hard to do with his heart galloping up his windpipe like a stampeding mustang. He wanted to leap on its back and get the hell out of there.

His hands itched to wrap themselves in her wild strawberry blond mane. But no wild mane flowed down the back of FBI Special Agent Kendall Barlow. It was pulled smoothly against her head into a ponytail. A few short tendrils escaped in front of her ears, the lobes pierced with the small diamond studs he'd given her.

"Nice to see you," she said, before smiling a strained grin.

"Hey." It felt awkward. He hadn't been alone with her in a long time. He deliberately eased his shoulders, trying to relax. "Nice earrings."

She fingered a stud, as if figuring out which pair she wore. "Oh, these? I can't remember where I got them."

She teased with a genuine smile now. She remembered exactly who had given them to her... Him.

The awkwardness was worth it for the smile he hadn't seen in months. "I... No one told me it was your task force."

"Can we sort through the conflict of interest after Mrs. Pelzel's interview? She's watching us out her window."

"Would you like to work with someone else?"

"Of course not." She stopped on the sidewalk, head tilted to the side to look up at him. Physically only an arm's length away, but completely out of his reach. "We can be professional about this. At least I can."

Professional? Sure. Why the hell not?

Her task force. Her lead. Her knock on the door. He turned sideways on the porch to let her pass. The slight scent of ginger and orange filled him with memories. He recognized the smell of her lotion and was getting sentimental. Instead of pulling her into his arms and kissing her until they were both senseless, he tugged off his dark shades and tucked them in his pocket.

He could be professional. If he had to.

Kendall explained who they were when Mrs. Pelzel came to the door. She introduced him as Ranger Murray. No one was the wiser that they were married, since she'd always used her maiden name professionally. Once they were invited inside, Heath quickly discovered Kendall had been on this case for several months. Sitting on one of the most uncomfortable couches in the world, he concentrated on Mrs. Pelzel preparing large glasses of iced tea. A suddenly dry throat couldn't wait to be quenched.

Kendall looked at a message on her phone, and he

wondered how they'd drifted apart. More than five years of his life had been devoted to this woman.

How could it all be gone over one wrong question? He didn't want it to be. But getting back to her wouldn't be easy.

Once again, he was close enough to touch his wife, but promise bound to keep it professional. Reminding himself to stay professional. He'd kept that way back when they'd first met. He could do it again now.

Mrs. Pelzel brought the glasses in on a tray. He popped off the couch to help, but she shrugged him off. "Please sit. I have never had a real Texas Ranger visit before. This is so exciting."

She handed them each a glass. He downed his in record time and could only blame it on nerves.

Kendall set down her glass after taking a sip, then straightened her jacket. Time for business. "Mrs. Pelzel, would you be willing to let my computer forensics team take a look at the PC?"

"Can they do that from here? I don't think I could live without my computer for a long period of time," the home owner replied. "That's how I stay in touch with my grandkids, you know."

"We could have someone out here in a couple of days," he answered. "They could check it right here."

The older woman shook her head. "Oh, wait. You know, I should have told you when you first arrived. There's really not a problem, so you'd be wasting your time."

Kendall gave him a look he should have been able to interpret. Maybe she'd just been surprised that he'd given an answer she didn't like. Maybe she thought it strange that Mrs. Pelzel had changed her mind. He didn't know, and that was disappointing since he should, being her husband and all.

"Mrs. Pelzel, what happened that made you call the FBI?" Kendall asked. Her notebook was open. Her pen was clicked to a ready position, but her casual body language told him she wasn't expecting a real answer.

That hadn't changed, at least. He could still read her mannerisms, it seemed.

"I'm afraid I'm just a silly old ninny who made a mistake," the older woman said.

Kendall turned a page in her notebook, sliding her finger across the handwriting as she skimmed the page. "You told us you had a feeling that someone was watching you through the computer's camera."

"I did," the older woman whispered.

To her credit, Kendall the FBI agent didn't roll her eyes or make any facial movement that indicated she didn't believe the older woman. "You also mentioned that the computer seemed to be running slower since they installed the Public Exposure gadget."

"Really, you should believe me when I tell you I made a mistake," Mrs. Pelzel said, her fingers twisting into the loose long-sleeved shirt she wore.

"Will you confirm that you have one of the PE monitoring systems?" Kendall's enthusiasm moved her forward to the edge of the couch. Both sets of law enforcement eyes moved toward the desk, where the older model computer sat.

"They seem like a legitimate company," he said, attempting to get Mrs. Pelzel to share more information.

"I'm not a helpless old woman who doesn't know

how to research a product or service. I didn't think it was anyone's business how much time I spent online. But the money they offered was enough to buy a new roof. I just couldn't pass that up."

He'd heard of Public Exposure and their controversial social media monitoring system. The file he'd been sent from the task force stated a strong belief the group was involved in more than the good of the common man.

"I sound old and kooky about someone watching me. But I swear that the camera light comes on by itself while I'm cooking or watching television. I hear a click, and the red light pops on and off." She covered her mouth like she'd said something wrong and then looked at her computer.

Warning bells sounded, and he couldn't help glancing over to see if the light was on.

"It doesn't sound kooky at all, Mrs. Pelzel," Kendall comforted. "In fact, we've had several other residents report the same thing. But we need to take your computer to our forensic team and have them check—"

"I'm sorry. Maybe I'll have my granddaughter look at it. I was wrong to bring you here. There's nothing weird going on." Mrs. Pelzel stood and lifted her hand toward her front door. "I'm sorry, but there's nothing I can do."

"Mrs. Pelzel, I believe you," Heath said. "A start to resolving this issue would be to make certain you log out of your Wi-Fi. Turn everything off before closing the lid and unplugging it. And ask your granddaughter to verify your router has an encryption key. You might want to change your password."

"Thank you. I'll try to remember, and I'm very sorry to have wasted your time."

Kendall stood, defeat written clearly on her face. She flipped her notebook closed and stowed it away inside her suit jacket. They both stopped on the front walk when the door shut. Heath squinted at the noon sun and put his glasses on while she made a couple of more notes.

"The precautions won't make any difference," Kendall told him, following with her sunglasses dangling from between her fingers.

"You don't think this is someone trying to steal identities, like that file sitting in my car states."

"It's bigger than that." Kendall continued to her car.

"How many reports have you taken?"

"Dozens." Kendall leaned on the government-issued sedan, appearing more defeated now than she had inside the house. "And for every person who reports that their camera light is sporadically coming on, there are probably another dozen who don't."

"It's a shame she wouldn't let an expert search her computer. But if you have had that many complaints, why haven't your FBI computer whizzes found what you need from those victims?" He crossed his arms across his chest and leaned his hip against the sedan, close to her.

"What did you think of Public Exposure before this morning?"

"I've seen their public service announcements. They're a group that promotes kids playing outside instead of hanging on social media. How are they involved in potential identity theft?"

"First, no accounts have been affected—bank, credit card or otherwise. None of these complaints go further than what you witnessed. Mrs. Pelzel doesn't realize that it was me who she spoke with when she called. I take the complaints, but by the time I get to an interview, something has changed their minds and they've all made a mistake."

"All of them?"

"This makes over twenty. Oh, and they all use the word *kooky*."

"They can't all be saying the same thing. You think Public Exposure is threatening them?"

"Yes. Sometime between when the resident calls me and when I get here. All of these people withdraw their complaints or concerns and I can't move forward."

Mrs. Pelzel watched them from her window. Heath saw her drop the curtain back into place. Without moving his head, he looked at the windows of the neighbors. More than one resident peered through the blinds.

"I kind of understand about that feeling of being watched." He barely nodded, but Kendall picked up what he was throwing down.

"There's also a white van at the end of the block." She pointed a finger behind her.

He glanced in that direction. "Two men in the front seat. Just sitting like they were when I arrived."

"Want another chat?"

"I'm game."

Kendall flipped her identification wallet open and held it in her left hand, leaving her right ready to react. Her weapon was at the ready in her shoulder harness, his at his hip. She turned and they took the first steps into the middle of the street toward the van.

The engine sprang to life and the van burned rubber

in reverse. It was around the corner before they could pivot and get back to the car.

"I didn't see a front license plate," Kendall said, pointing for him to get into her vehicle.

"Nope. At least we don't have to wonder if we're being watched or not." He hesitated to open her sedan's door. "My truck is faster than this old heap."

"Yeah, but this is government insured. I'd hate for our rates to go up."

He jumped inside and buckled up. That was his Kendall. Always practical.

And he loved it.

Chapter Four

Kendall concentrated on driving the car. If she let herself get distracted and think about why Heath had been assigned her case, she'd screw up. Driving or talking... somehow she'd messed up one or the other, and he'd shut down.

At the moment, his hand gripped the back of her seat and the other gripped the dash. He'd lowered the window as soon as she'd pulled away from Mrs. Pelzel's home.

"Do you see them?"

"You're about to cross Inwood. Take a right." He was grinning from ear to ear.

A definite improvement from when she'd first arrived. She'd thought he was about to throw up when Mrs. Pelzel went for the tea. She turned right as he suggested with the direction his finger pointed. For a by-the-book kind of guy, he had a good intuition about where criminals went.

"Slow down, Kendall." Heath dropped his hand and pulled his sidearm.

She tapped the brakes and followed the direction of his narrowed eyes, toward the end of the block where the van sat parked in a driveway. She couldn't tell if it actually belonged there or not. She slowed further.

"We need a better view." He rested his weapon on his thigh but kept it pointed toward his door.

"Do you think they've seen us?" She pulled the car to the curb, keeping her foot on the brake and the car in gear.

"Not sure."

"Thoughts?"

"They aren't getting out. We should call for backup. Last thing we need is a chase through a residential part of Dallas."

"Agreed. A high-speed chase isn't ideal anywhere."

"Nope."

At least he was concise. Shoot, he always had been. Heath Murray was a cowboy of few words.

"As soon as I put the car in Park, they'll take off."

"Probably. Backup?"

"I hate to do that when all we have is the suspicion they were watching us or Pelzel's house." She needed proof. Something solid to move forward with. Not a reprimand about pursuing innocent bystanders.

"They did peel out in Reverse to get away."

"True, but we hadn't identified ourselves. I just see a media nightmare when they claim we were coming at them with guns."

"Want me to ask?" His hand reached to open his door.

"Let's just wait a minute and see what they do."

She had no more than finished the sentence when two men exited the van, walked to the rear and removed paint buckets. One of the guys went and punched the doorbell, also knocking loud enough to send every dog on the block into a barkfest.

"You've got to be kidding me." She hit the steering wheel with the palms of both hands. "This is the first nibble I've had."

"Drive slow."

Kendall didn't hesitate and put the car in motion. With his gun resting on his thigh, Heath used his phone as a camera. She didn't have to watch. She was confident that he'd capture as many images as possible. She focused her gaze on the men, switching between them, watching for a weapon or any questionable movement.

They drew even with the house and the man still at the van climbed inside and quickly shut the rear doors. The one at the house knocked again, causing the dog inside to bark once more. She could see it bouncing against the window trying to get out.

"Catch the plate?" Heath asked.

"He stacked paint cans in front of it." Frustrated, she kept the car moving and pulled around the corner.

"We could wait here. See what they do."

"We'll give it a try." She performed a three-point turn, pulled next to the curb and cut the engine.

"Video call me." He plugged a headset into his phone and used one earpiece, dropping the phone into his jacket pocket. "Stay here."

"Heath, no." This went against training, but it was their best option.

"Don't worry. I don't do crazy." With those words, he was out of the car and tapping the hood as he walked around the front.

She should have been more insistent and demand he

return to the car. She dialed and he answered but didn't talk. She could hear his boots on the street, his breathing and then the echo of street sounds after she heard them in real time.

He crossed the street and stood on the grass at the corner house's garage wall. The cell screen finally showed a picture other than the inside of his pocket. He lifted the phone around the corner, and she could see past the neighboring driveways.

"They're standing at the back of the van. One's talking pretty rapidly and waving his hands. Can you make out what they're saying? I can't."

"No," he whispered into his microphone.

"They're both looking in your direction, but I don't think they can see the phone. The driver is opening the doors and putting the paint back inside."

"I can have a conversation," he whispered.

"No. Heath, no. Just wait." She had a bad feeling. A very bad feeling.

Trusting premonitions had never been a strategy for her. She never looked for good luck or blamed a bad streak on chance. More than anything else, she investigated and found the answers through old-fashioned hard work.

But something screamed at her to get Heath back in the car.

"Time to pack it up, Heath."

The screen went black as she heard the driver slam the van doors shut in real time and then on the echo in the video delay. She started the car to be at the ready.

But Heath didn't return to the vehicle. She inched the car forward until she could see her husband disappearing into the front door alcove, getting closer to the van instead of coming back to her.

"Heath!" She called to him without any response. She sank lower in her seat, hoping neither man in the van noticed the car.

The van's engine roared to life.

Kendall braced herself, fairly certain that the next thing she heard would be gunfire. The van peeled out of the driveway and down the street…toward her, passing Heath and turning left. Perfect for them to follow.

"Let's go!" Heath's voice roared at her through the phone.

She put the car into Drive, stopping just as he rushed away from the house and leapt over a small hedge. Even in boots, Heath was across the concrete street and in the car within seconds.

His speed always amazed her. Riding horses, running or taking down a suspect…the action didn't matter. His hat was in his lap, and his hands were waving to follow the van.

"We don't really have a reason to follow these guys," she mentioned as she took the next left, back to the main road they'd turned from earlier. "Why do you want to pursue?"

"Gut feeling?"

Just as she was about to open her mouth to explain how their joint task force operated—that she was in charge and he shouldn't take off like he had—the van sped up and fishtailed around a corner.

"If they really think that's going to work, I guess they don't know much about you, Kendall."

Even increasing their speed and darting around a

car, she caught the smile and wink. The natural response was to smile back. So she did. It was the reason she'd fallen in love with him. His gallantry. His bravery. His…okay, everything.

Kendall stopped herself, concentrating on switching lanes and accelerating. She'd confront him later. After whatever they were doing was over.

"Watch out." Heath raised his voice, pointing in front of them.

The van went through a yellow light. They weren't running sirens. And a powder-pink sedan, heading in the opposite direction, turned left in front of them. They were going to hit each other. Kendall slammed on her brakes, as did the sedan. They barely avoided each other as they fishtailed sideways to a stop.

"Gun it. Car to your left."

She heard the words and trusted the Texas Ranger next to her. She floored the gas, trying to look for crossing traffic, getting their car across the intersection. It was a good time of day to be on Northwest Highway. No one was in their path when she heard brakes from one direction and tires squealing from the other.

The SUV they'd passed a few seconds earlier had crashed into the rear of the pink car, stopping where her sedan would have been if Heath hadn't yelled. There was a loud bang and horns.

"Great job, babe." Heath patted her shoulder from where he rested his arm along the back of her seat. "I'll check on the drivers."

She pulled around to protect the drivers from oncoming traffic and hit the hazard lights. Heath got out, leaving his hat in his seat. She dropped her head to the wheel, reaching for her phone to call the accident in to authorities and request a tow truck. She sat back as she gave all the appropriate information, letting out a long sigh.

The van was out of sight. Heath was busy with the drivers, and all Kendall could do was force herself to breathe. That had been close. Too close.

No suspect was worth what had almost happened. She had to be more careful, less reckless. Skylar Dawn needed her parents to come home. Period.

"You okay?" Heath asked, back at the passenger door.

She nodded, still a little stunned by it all.

"I can't say I'm bummed about them getting away." The corner of his mouth barely rose as he leaned on the car.

"What? Why's that?"

"Where's the fun in catching them the first day I get to work with you again?"

He said it with such a straight face that if she hadn't known him, she never would've seen that playful gleam in his eye. Yet she couldn't argue with the logic either. She would've been bummed, too.

Chapter Five

Heath wanted to take Kendall in his arms until she stopped shaking, but he'd jumped out of the car to check on the other drivers. Instead of helping her now, he spoke to her through the passenger door, keeping the entire front seat between them.

Hugging your wife after an accident was allowed, in his book. He just didn't know if it fell under the professional umbrella. He straightened, grabbing his aching ribs, worse now because of slamming into the seat belt. But he swallowed the grimace of pain, keeping it to himself. He wouldn't mention it to the EMTs who would be arriving on the scene, judging by the distant sirens.

Kendall stretched a couple of times as she stood from the car. "I can't believe they missed us."

"You didn't hesitate."

She nodded, letting the statement stand as a compliment about their teamwork. And this time, he didn't add the frightening picture in his head of a different outcome. If she had stopped to question why he was yelling a command at her... Damn, they would be pinned between those two cars right now.

But she hadn't. They were unharmed. Fine to go

home to Skylar Dawn. And good enough to work together tomorrow.

"The drivers are fine." He'd walked around the hood of the car before realizing it. His hand opened between Kendall's shoulder blades, and he might have patted her a couple of times if he hadn't seen the tears.

But he had.

Just two, but they were enough to make her curl into the crook of his arm and stand there until they heard the first siren grow close. She broke away like someone had thrown water on them.

"Traffic needs to get through. I should probably move the car." Her voice was awkward and strained as she looked around the intersection.

"I can take care of it."

"Don't coddle me, Heath."

"Whoa there, *partner.*" He emphasized the last word to remind her why they were there. "I'm allocating resources. You're the better photographer. I'm going to need every angle possible before the cars move." He stuck his hand in his pocket.

Her mouth formed a perfect O before accepting his phone. Then she was back. Professional. Doing her job as the authorities arrived. Identifying herself as an agent and taking pictures.

Staying out of the way, the Dallas PD officer gave him the go-ahead to move the FBI sedan. It didn't have a scratch on it. Just as he opened the door, in a moment where no one else watched, he caught a glance between the two drivers.

A knowing glance. Like they'd gotten away with something.

It took him a few minutes to get the sedan back on

the same side of the street as the rest of the cars. By the time he returned, both drivers stood with officers, giving their statements. After an initial check, they'd both declined the ambulance ride to a hospital.

The woman in the pink car was crying again, her mascara smeared like his mother-in-law's the day his world had turned upside down. It was hard not to think about it—the afternoon Skylar Dawn had broken her arm. But he pushed it from his mind.

Something was off about the accident. Maybe he'd been hanging around Wade too much lately. His friend's intuition seemed to be rubbing off on him. Everything about the SUV guy who had nearly T-boned them screamed that the man wanted to run.

It had to be the highway patrol officer in him. He'd stopped more than his fair share of antsy drivers with drugs or weapons in their cars. The SUV driver shifted his weight from foot to foot. He kept looking around, especially at Kendall.

Okay, Heath admitted that his wife was an extremely attractive woman. Nothing about her shouted married or mom. And seeing her work again was…hot. He got why men would watch her. But this guy didn't have a look like he was trying to ask her out.

Nope. Heath recognized the short glances. The slow quarter turns to keep her in his peripheral vision. The driver must not realize that Heath was a Ranger or anyone else significant. He hadn't given him a second glance since Heath asked if he was okay.

Heath leaned against the pink car's trunk, watching both the drivers through his mirrored shades. There it was again. A specific look that acknowledged the drivers knew each other. One of the man's eyebrows rose, and the woman's chin lifted slightly.

Indiscernible to anyone not watching them specifically. A look that confirmed his gut feeling that something was off. If he'd looked away for a split second, he would have missed it.

If the drivers knew each other, they must know the men in the white van. He took a step toward Kendall, who was wrapping up with the officers. But what would he tell her?

That his instinct told him these two apparently innocent victims had a connection to the group Kendall was looking into? They couldn't hold the two based on his observation. His gut instinct had gotten them into this accident by encouraging her to follow the van.

If he followed any intuition, it would be to keep his thoughts and observations to himself until they could investigate. That's what the Rangers and FBI did. They found the facts and built cases.

He'd wait.

For now, he'd make it clear about his role here. No reason to let Public Exposure know he was working with Kendall. He pushed off the trunk and marched to Kendall's side. He pulled her close to him.

When she turned to him—most likely to express her anger—he kissed her. A full-on-the-mouth, like-she-belonged-to-him kiss. For the moment…she did. Although she may not after the next time they were alone.

"I'll explain when we're alone," he whispered. Then in a louder voice, "You ready to go, babe?"

He could see the fury rising for him embarrassing

her. "Gentlemen." She nodded to the officers, excusing herself.

Heath didn't back off. He kept his arm around Kendall's waist as they walked to her sedan. He opened her door and tried to kiss her again.

"No way," she said, dodging his attempt. "You better have a dang good reason for what you just did."

He ran around the back of the car, trying to come up with something. Anything other than the real reason, since he didn't want to explain himself. At least not yet.

She stared at him as he snapped his seat belt into place.

"Well?"

"It was time to go."

She huffed. "That makes no sense at all. If you wanted to go, you could have said something and not embarrassed me in front of the Dallas PD."

He let her vent as he looked through the pictures she'd taken of the scene. Once he was back in the office, he'd be able to run a full background check. Once he had information, he'd explain to Kendall.

"You aren't listening to me."

"What?"

Kendall slowed to a stop beside his truck. "I said, if you're going to get possessive because someone's looking at me, then this joint effort isn't going to work."

"That wasn't… I wasn't…" he tried. *Get your information right before you tell her.* "Professional. Got it."

The awkward pause resulted in an awkward thumb gesture indicating he should get out of the car. She lowered the passenger window from her side and waited until he bent his face down to look at her.

"I'll talk to you tonight when you call Skylar Dawn. We'll decide what our next move is and where to meet tomorrow."

"Good idea."

He stood. The window went up and she pulled away, leaving him in the middle of the street. She had a right to be upset. On the surface, he'd behaved badly.

Back in his truck, he resisted the impulse to bang the dashboard. It sure didn't appear that he'd racked up any points for moving back home. He'd do his research, and maybe his instinct about the drivers would pay off.

Drapes dropped into place at the house to his left. Blinds closed at Mrs. Pelzel's home. There was more to this case than fraud. Every instinct he possessed told him so. Kendall was keeping something from him. He knew that before being assigned to her task force.

Fraud? Or a decision about their life—together or apart? Maybe helping his wife would give them an opportunity to really talk. But now, it was time to work some computer magic to figure out what secrets the residents of Hall Street were keeping.

Chapter Six

"If I weren't a mom, I'd be cussing like a sailor right now." Kendall closed the office door behind her.

Jerry Fisher didn't look up from the paperwork under his pen. "I put in the request as you asked. You must have known there was a possibility that your husband would continue on the task force until they could find an alternate. Do I need to file a furgle conflict of interest and pull you from the case? Oh, sorry. I forgot you're offended by that word."

The witty comeback she'd expected hadn't come. Instead he'd deliberately used that stupid word. Her supervisor sounded…bothered. *Shoot.* She'd been using his listening abilities for her personal venting. That needed to stop.

The pen dropped to the desk, and he covered the papers with a file. Kendall plopped down in the lone chair near the bookshelf, emotionally exhausted. She'd only returned to the office to delay explaining to her mother why she looked like she hadn't slept in a year.

Jerry leaned back in his chair, fingers locked casually behind his neck. "Look, if it's too difficult to work with Murray, I can give this thing to Kilpatrick. It'll die a quick death, and it won't be your responsibility or be on your record."

"Kilpatrick is two months away from retirement. He won't take it seriously." She could handle Heath and the investigation. If she couldn't…well, she deserved to be reassigned.

"We both know this investigation isn't going anywhere, Kendall. I spoke with my supervisor and the DC cybercrime group supervisor. They're still not interested until your victims have monetary losses or receive extortion threats. It's just not a priority for them." He leaned forward, chatting like the friend he'd been when they'd first started out at the Bureau. More like he was doing her a favor by taking the case away.

Did he really believe she was wasting her time? Had he lost confidence in her ability? Or was her desire to crack a big case obscuring the reality that Public Exposure wasn't one?

"We actually had a break this afternoon. The address of the complaint was being watched by two men." She wouldn't remind him that she could manage Heath.

The fact was that Jerry Fisher drank the Kool-Aid. He'd moved up to management. He was her boss. Bosses lived by the rules. Bosses wanted successful investigations. Bosses didn't need to hear about personal problems.

If he needed results…well, that's what she'd give him.

"Were you able to question them?" He picked up the pen and tapped both ends back and forth on the manila folder.

"We were in pursuit when they— No. No questioning, yet." But the incident strengthened her resolve. She was on to something important. "I won't take up any more of your time."

"Furgle. I have time." He gestured to the files on his desk. "Believe me, I'd rather be in the field with you again."

"I bet." She smiled, in spite of his using that stupid word…again. She left more determined than ever to break this case wide open.

Jerry wasn't the only one who needed results. Climbing the FBI ladder had been her dream for as long as she could remember. She needed a big win in her column. Someday she wanted to be the agent in charge, the boss, the person others reported to.

But, honestly, she couldn't remember why.

Did she want to be behind a desk making all the decisions without the full picture? Did she want to move and take Skylar Dawn away from her life here? And, more importantly, away from her father?

Like my mother did?

God, the realization stopped her in her tracks. That wasn't the plan when their argument started. Well, marrying and having a child had never been a part of her life plan either. She rubbed her palms together as she continued down the hallway. She needed to reevaluate her life. The realization wasn't a surprise. She just hadn't admitted it to herself before this minute.

Even though she'd wanted to have the same evaluation talk with Heath, she hadn't acknowledged it was exactly what she needed to do personally.

She needed more information about Public Exposure, which would mean a late night of research. But her first call was to the house. Her mother picked up

Skylar Dawn from day care each day, but she always waited until Kendall got home before serving dinner.

"Mommy!" her daughter answered. She either could recognize the caller ID or knew it wasn't six o'clock and time for Heath's call.

"Hey, sweetheart. How did today go?"

"Bumble the rabbit died, Mommy. It's so sad. I'll miss her."

"That is sad, honey. Is your class all right?"

"Yeah, Miss Darinda says it's part of the circle of life. Like the lion movie."

"That's true."

"I drew a picture. MiMi put it on the frigeator."

"I'll be sure to look at it when I get home."

Skylar Dawn sighed long and very audibly into the receiver. "Working late again? My, my, my."

Her daughter mimicked frequent sayings of the adults around her. This particular one was used by Naomi in an attempt to make Kendall feel guilty or ashamed. Kendall already felt both, since she'd be missing time at home.

"Yes, sweet pea. I'm working late, but I'll be home in time to read a chapter from our book."

"I could get Daddy to read it."

God, she felt guilty enough without letting Heath know she was working late on a Monday. Tuesdays and Thursdays were normally spent in the office. That was Heath's night at the house. For some stupid reason, she didn't want him to know that the late hours were extending to other days of the week.

"I'll be home in time. Can you get MiMi?"

"Love you, bye-bye."

Maybe it was superwoman syndrome or imposter syndrome or some other syndrome working mothers had come up with. Whatever it was could be added to the list of things she needed to face and talk about with Heath.

Not Jerry. Not her mother. And not any other friend or coworker.

It was time she admitted she couldn't do everything.

Right after she proved that Public Exposure wasn't what they claimed.

HEATH'S PHONE ALARM SOUNDED. Five minutes until his six o'clock phone call. He swiped open the book, getting it ready to read for Skylar Dawn.

"Barlow residence."

Naomi. Not the cheerful voice of his daughter.

"Evening, Naomi. May I speak with Skylar Dawn?"

"I'm sorry, Heath. She's taking her bath. She got exceptionally dirty this afternoon hopping around like a bunny." Naomi described the playful act with disgust.

"Is Kendall available, or is she in with her?"

"She's not here tonight."

"And after Skylar Dawn's done?"

"Returning your call is not my responsibility, Heath."

"Gotcha. She's being punished for getting dirty." He waited, but Naomi didn't respond. "At least tell her I called?"

Again there was silence.

If Heath hung up, it would be the only part of the conversation repeated to Kendall. He kept the line open, waiting until his mother-in-law responded. In fact, he put the call on speaker and looked at the book.

He heard splashing and singing in the background. Naomi had returned to the bathroom.

"I can't stay on the phone any longer. It's time to wash her hair." She disconnected.

"I think Naomi Barlow is in contention for the monster-in-law of the year award," Wade Hamilton stated without looking across the office at Heath.

"Mind your own business. Wait. That's impossible for you, right?"

"I was commiserating with you, man. I know what that phone call means to you."

"You're as bad as an old meddling matchmaker. Admit it. You're the one who assigned me to Kendall's task force." He swiveled in his chair to face Wade.

No one else was in the office. He could speak freely. He had intended not to mention the conflict-of-interest part of his assignment. His anger was actually at his mother-in-law and the phone call. He should shut up. Keep it to himself—his general policy about everything these days.

Too late now.

Wade took a few seconds to smile like a cat skimming a bucket of milk still under the cow. Then he rolled his pen between his palms, shrugging his shoulders slightly.

"I'm not sure if I should slug you or thank you."

"Hey, I'm just looking out for my own self-interests here," Wade said, spinning back to his computer screen. "I'm tired of hearing Slate complain about your bad habits."

"I have a few stories I could tell."

He held up his hand. "God, no. I have no reason to

listen to more. Instead, is there anything I can help you with?"

"Thanks, but no. I'm running some facial recognitions and backgrounds. Why aren't you going home?"

Wade shrugged again. "I have my own demons to chase."

Demons? Heath recognized barriers. Several months ago Wade had been brutally beaten, cracking ribs and almost losing an eye. He would have lost his life if it hadn't been for a woman named Therese Ortis warning another company Ranger, Jack MacKinnon.

All traces of the woman had vaporized. Was she the demon Wade chased? Too late to ask. The conversation was over.

It was a good time to step outside and call Kendall. He left a message when she didn't answer, then texted her to call when she was home so he could talk with Skylar Dawn. The light pollution around here didn't block every star in the sky. He perched against the tailgate and just looked out.

There would be rain in the next couple of days. The color around the moon had changed. His mother had taught him that. He should take his daughter for a visit. Soon. But the nine-hour drive to Southwest Texas was hard enough when two parents shared the responsibilities.

That had been the excuse, and his parents had accepted it. The last real trip they'd taken to Alpine had slowed them down further with the horse trailer to pick up Jupitar and Stardust almost a year ago. When had life gotten out of hand?

The day I walked out of my house.

Needing a pep talk, he dialed. "Hey, Mom. How's everything going?"

"It's much the same. The baseball team looks to do pretty good this year. But you didn't call to catch up on Sul Ross."

"I don't mind hearing about it." And he didn't. Just listening to his mom's voice gave him a sense of inner calm.

"Are you still living…?"

"At the Thompson ranch? Yes. And no, I haven't really talked to Kendall. Skylar Dawn is growing and getting more amazing every day. She made new paintings for everyone. I'll get it in the mail this weekend."

"No rodeo? No busting heads?"

He rubbed his bruised ribs but knew his mother referred to Kendall's mom. "That was this past weekend. Okay, maybe it happened a little tonight, too."

"Uh-huh. You're going to kill yourself and make that woman very happy."

He was pretty sure he wouldn't drop dead, but the pain was a constant reminder that he might not have too many rodeo days left. Maybe he should focus on more rides with Skylar Dawn instead.

"Mom. We've talked about this. I need the money." Yeah, he did. And one crack about his mother-in-law was all either of them was allowed.

The extra work he did around the ranch still didn't repay the Thompsons what boarding his two horses would cost. He was determined to make up the difference and not accept a free ride.

"We could help you out, but you won't let us."

"You already have three full-time jobs. A professor at the university, a wife and a nurse to Dad. You're the one who needs to slow down. I should be sending money to you. Is he okay?"

"Dad is still the same. He's giving everyone what for, doesn't remember doing it, then does it again." She laughed. "I wish we could come see you, but breaking his routine is really hard."

"I know, Mom. I should be there."

"Nonsense. You have a very important job, a family and a wonderful daughter. Concentrate on those precious girls."

"Yes, ma'am."

"I'll call my grandbaby this weekend. You okay? I should get your daddy into bed soon."

"Just that…I'm always better after talking to you." His mother's positive, can-do attitude poured out of her every sentence. "Love you."

"I love you, too, son."

Talking to at least one woman he loved gave him his second wind. He returned to his desk and began the computer searches he needed on Public Exposure. He wanted to know everything.

Making a substantial contribution in the morning would make it much harder to stop his involvement with the case. The last thing he wanted was for Kendall to play the conflict-of-interest card.

Wade finally went home.

It was too late to speak with his daughter. Too late to read to her. He had no reason to text his wife. Again.

"This can't be right." The addresses of the two drivers today weren't only on the same street in Dallas—they were on the same block.

He looked up the owners—not them, a corporation.

Now the digging got fun. So fun he didn't notice the time until it was two in the morning.

Time to call it a night.

He had what he'd been searching for. A good, solid, old-fashioned lead.

Chapter Seven

Kendall opened the front door and found Heath leaning against her SUV. One hand held a donut with sprinkles, and the other had a large coffee. Skylar Dawn ran past in her pink jeans and matching jacket.

"Daddy!"

Heath set the coffee cup down on the hood and lifted their daughter to his hip. He received his hug and smooches, then set their almost-four-year-old on the ground.

"Is that for me?"

"Yepper doodles." He smiled like Kendall hadn't seen him smile in months. "Jump inside and buckle up first."

He opened the door, got Skylar Dawn settled inside and handed her the donut, complete with a set of napkins to cover her favorite blue bunny shirt she wore in honor of Bumble the rabbit.

Kendall stood there, finishing the last bit of coffee in her travel mug before setting it on the front porch. Without looking, she knew her mother disapproved behind the curtain. She didn't care.

Heath was a great father.

Their baby girl had cried herself to sleep the night before. The tearstains had been apparent on her plump little cheeks. It had been a rare occasion that Kendall hadn't made it home to tuck her into bed. Then she'd noticed her phone battery had gone dead. When she plugged it in, there were numerous messages from Heath.

They'd ranged from upset about her mother to extremely worried about where she was to wondering why she was ignoring him and offering to pull himself from the Public Exposure investigation. She'd texted that her phone had died and received a Great in response.

Of course it wasn't great. Their situation was far from great.

But watching him with their daughter made her knees melt. He showed so clearly how much he loved Skylar Dawn. It brought tears to her already puffy eyes. She hadn't slept. A recurring vision of what could have happened at that intersection had kept her awake most of the night.

"Come on, Mommy," Skylar Dawn said between bites.

"That better be a double shot, skim with a dash of vanilla," she answered from the porch before joining them.

"Why would I order you anything else?" He smiled at her, too.

But as he handed it to her, he glared at the window where the curtains moved slightly. She didn't blame him. Her mother had no right to decide Skylar Dawn shouldn't speak with her father.

That was a direction in which Kendall never wanted to head. No matter what happened between her and

Heath, their daughter would never be used to hurt him. She'd made both of those points clear to her mother as soon as they'd gotten up.

"How did you know to bring the donut this morning?" she whispered as she passed him.

"I had a hunch." He cut his eyes toward the window again.

"I did speak with her about bath time."

"Ha. Like that has ever worked before," he said to her over the SUV, then pulled at the booster seat straps to verify they were locked in place. "Mind if I ride in with you?"

Not waiting for an answer, he jumped in the passenger seat and buckled up.

He has a point.

Setting her mother straight hadn't ever done any good. The woman had a habit of behaving exactly how she pleased. Oh sure, her mother helped by picking up Skylar Dawn and spending the night whenever the job required late hours. But she never really let Kendall forget that she'd helped. Or that Naomi Barlow's way was probably the better one.

Explaining why Kendall did something a particular way didn't matter. Naomi just nodded and proceeded as she liked. It was something Kendall had accepted for years.

But not after last night.

Not after seeing her precious little girl's hitched breathing from crying in her sleep.

"It won't happen again, Heath," she said, buckling her belt. She meant it. And she'd told her mother as much.

He placed his hand over hers on the shifter. "Tell

Naomi that next time, she'll have to tell me to my face." His voice was low and carefully controlled.

They were all upset. Well, perhaps their daughter wasn't any longer. Her smile had white icing and rainbow sprinkles surrounding it.

"Is that good, sweet pea?" She changed the subject instead of reassuring Heath again.

Skylar Dawn nodded, holding out the now-icing-free donut. "Want a bite?"

"No thanks, Daddy brought me my own treat."

They drove to the day care, listening to stories of Bumble the rabbit. The kids had a memorial service planned for today. Kendall tried to concentrate, but her brain—and body—kept coming back to the surge of energy she'd felt when Heath's hand had covered hers.

The split second of comfort and reassurance had done crazy things to her emotions. She missed that feeling. Missed driving together. Missed family dinners.

Missed him.

This tsunami of emotions set her dangerously close to tears as Heath walked inside the day care with Skylar Dawn. She had only a few minutes to get herself together.

Turn off the emotions. Turn on professionalism. Think professionally.

"Man, those kids are taking this bunny thing seriously," he said, getting back into the car.

Kendall pulled through the drive and was back on a major street before she tried to think of something to say. But her mind was blank. Wiped spotless like a counter top after her mother had cleaned.

"Find anything by working late last night?" he asked.

Professional.

"I eliminated possibilities, but haven't found anything specific."

"I worked late, too." His voice held a subtle tease that she recognized.

"How could you find something on the first day?"

"I didn't want to speculate yesterday. But I kept getting the feeling that the drivers of the other cars knew each other."

"I totally missed that."

"You were kind of shaken up."

A professional wouldn't admit that she'd been shaken up all night. "Did they know each other?"

"It goes beyond that. They're both members of Public Exposure. Have been for about three years."

Six years ago, she had slammed on the brakes and hugged him after a similar announcement. It had broken the ice, and after their joint case was over, they'd gone on a date. Then another and another.

"It's hard to believe they'd be that bold and try to…to…"

"Kill us? They probably would have liked those results." He took out his phone. "I have their address. They live on the same block off Wycliff, near Uptown."

Genuine excitement. They might be getting a break. She headed the SUV in the general direction that would take them north of downtown Dallas. New nightclubs and restaurants were springing up in the area all the time. Housing was sort of limited and in high demand, barely keeping up.

"You got a lot accomplished last night."

"There's more. They were both convicted of fraud. The Postal Inspection Service brought charges that stuck. The guy's still on probation. He'll see his probation officer next week."

"Why didn't you mention this yesterday? I could have saved you time and run it through the FBI database."

"I got what we needed," he said, pointing out a left turn. "I could just as easily have been wrong and wasted the whole night."

"But you weren't. This might just be the break we needed."

"Are you going to tell me why you feel so strongly about this case? What made you think there's more to it?"

"Maybe I had a hunch myself."

She couldn't admit she needed something big for her next promotion. Or that the promotion might result in a transfer. Not after the night they'd all just had. She wasn't prepared to have that conversation yet. Talk about counting chickens before they hatch.

She glanced at him during a stop light. He was waiting, patiently. Good grief, wasn't there anything bad about the man? Oh yeah, he wanted her to quit her job.

"It bugged me that this antisocial group would be paying people to monitor their social media use. Where's all the money coming from for their so-called study?"

"Have you checked on that?"

"One fund. They actually told me about that."

"You've interviewed them? Been to their offices?"

"I actually made a phone call. I don't have enough to subpoena their financial records. Maybe they thought if they told me, I'd give up."

"But it just made you more curious."

"Exactly."

"If there was an actual social media study, they'd have a variety of participants. Almost all of the people who were accepted are over the age of sixty. They're almost all single-person households and all homeowners."

"I noticed that, too. Wouldn't you want to target social media users under thirty? I mean, if you're trying to change the world and want less use. Why such weird participants? That's what piqued my curiosity. Then I found the odd complaint about being watched or feeling like they were being watched."

"What do you think is going on? You ruled out identity theft, but what else could it be?"

"That was my first guess. But the participants haven't lost money. At least not that they'll admit to me. They receive their payments from the study. I suspect that Public Exposure has a bigger plan. I just can't determine what direction to even look."

"Remember—whatever they're doing, it's big enough to want you out of the way. They must think you're on to something."

Yesterday's car incident came rushing back. "I could have gotten both of us killed."

"It was my fault, babe. I was the one who wanted to follow the van." His palm covered her upper arm, then slid up and down comfortingly before he pulled it back across the console.

"No one's to blame. I appreciate you checking them out. Seriously. Now we have a lead."

"A definite connection to Public Exposure, like you suspected." He adjusted in his seat, looking antsy and uncomfortable.

She turned the SUV a couple of times and realized they were a few minutes away from their destination. She hadn't gone by the office to verify information or follow any of her normal procedures of obtaining another vehicle. The excitement of working with Heath today and all his information had totally distracted her from her normal routine.

Even the drama at home this morning couldn't take away from the excitement of working with this particular Texas Ranger. He believed her. He trusted her instincts.

She stopped and shifted the car into Park with two blocks to go.

"You got me so excited about advancing the case, I forgot to pick up a Bureau car."

"Well, damn. There's not room for them both with Skylar Dawn's booster seat back there." He joked as if he hadn't been waiting for her to figure that out on her own.

He'd never chance someone discovering what car they drove. Neither would she. They'd have to go back. Fortunately, they weren't far from the field office.

"Look, Heath. I might have suggested that I'm totally in charge here. But that shouldn't stop you from sharing your ideas and consulting with me."

"Tell me what you need, Kendall. I'm at your service."

"Advice. Honest advice, not just what I want to hear. Last night my supervisor was getting in my head, making me wonder if this was truly worth pursuing."

The truth of her words didn't scare her. It felt good to say them out loud.

"Last night you didn't know these people had tried to kill you."

"They tried to kill you, too."

He pressed his lips together and shook his head. "I'm pretty certain they didn't know I was on the case with you. They might now, but yesterday was all about you."

"You're probably right about that." She hesitated to mention the panicked feelings she had the day before, but if they were working together, maybe he should know. But the words didn't form.

"Head to your office. Arrange for backup. Then we can bring both of the drivers in for an interview."

Was he asking a question or giving her a suggestion?

"Why do I get the feeling that you aren't going with me?"

"I don't mind taking a walk and keeping an eye on things until you get back."

"No. You're right. We honestly don't know how these people are going to react. They tried to kill us, Heath. What would happen to Skylar Dawn?"

"I see your point. We wouldn't want your mother raising her." He followed up with a laugh.

Heath had always been honest with her. Even though he'd chuckled, hard truth echoed in his words. Their daughter could not end up an orphan.

"You asked me for my honest opinion, Kendall. I gave it to you." He turned in the seat, picking up his hat from next to the car seat in back.

"You are not going out there on your own."

"I'm just going to verify the suspects are home. Just a little old-fashioned Ranger surveillance while you get things settled. If I have a problem, I'll call Jack. He's close by on assignment."

He opened his door.

"Call Jack on the way. You knock. I'll have your back from the street."

"Good idea. Let's go."

He winked at her like that had been his plan all along.

Chapter Eight

Heath made the call to Jack while on their walk around the corner. His voice sounded normal, no overreaction, no urgency. But Kendall could feel the readiness in his determined steps. In the way he moved his badge from his shirt to his suit coat. And in the way he flipped that same jacket behind his holster.

She clicked the lock button on her key ring, and the horn echoed off the gas station behind it. She looked down the block at an array of businesses on Lemmon Avenue, then back in the direction they were heading—full of renovated homes and thirty-year-old apartment buildings. Truly one of the up-and-coming parts of Dallas. One side of the street had gated driveways with stairs leading up to the front doors. The other side had parking along the street.

"This isn't a good place to follow someone," she mumbled since Heath was still talking to Jack.

"I texted the address," he said into the phone. "Yeah, we headed straight here instead of picking up a government issue. Right. No way we're letting them get a look at Kendall's regular ride. Skylar Dawn's seat is in the back…Six minutes is great. We'll be at the corner."

Six minutes. They could wait six minutes. The drivers from the previous day didn't know they were coming. Together with Heath, she could observe, make a plan, get prepared, call her office for backup.

"I can't believe I totally forgot to grab a sedan," she said once he was off the phone.

"We were talking, no big deal. Jack won't be long. This may turn out to be nothing."

Waiting on one of Heath's fellow Rangers would give them time to collaborate. But each minute ticked by excruciatingly slowly. And quietly. The more time she spent observing their surroundings, the less she felt like talking. Heath sent the pictures and information about the two suspects to her phone. She had a good image of who they were looking for.

"Good idea." She tilted her phone's screen toward him. "I can barely remember anything about how they look. Saundra Rosa and Bryan Marrone. I didn't give them a second thought."

"You can't do everything, Kendall. Even though you get close every day."

"Thanks," she whispered. Partly because she wasn't good at accepting praise and partly because of the weird feeling the neighborhood gave her.

Four more minutes.

"About this thing with your mother…"

Heath raised his hat and pushed his longer-than-normal hair back from his forehead. Then he secured his official white hat once again. It was one of his common stall tactics, waiting for her to explain or offer an excuse for Naomi. Then he wouldn't have to talk. But there was no excuse.

"It was wrong and uncalled-for. I told her as much." She did a three-sixty checking the neighborhood again. "Isn't it kind of weird that no one's around? Not a single person."

"You noticed that, too?"

"Do you feel this?" She twirled her finger in the air. "It's like that time at Fright Fest when the zombies were following me."

"Actually, watching you there was a lot of fun for me. But I know what you mean."

"You're getting that prickly sensation like someone's watching you?"

"That would be an affirmative." His voice lowered as his right hand descended to rest on his weapon. "You noticing a theme with these houses?"

They passed Rawlins Street heading to the next block.

"Either they all used the same bucket of paint for their trim…" She counted two houses without the same color. Heath kept walking but managed to turn in a full circle, checking their backs.

"Or they're all owned by the same corporation, which has an odd color preference." Most of the house trim looked the same as the apartment windows from the previous block. She'd seen that specific color every day recently in her files. "Unless you're really into Public Exposure orange."

"You think everyone who uses that color are members? Maybe it's a home owners' association thing." He shrugged. "Maybe they're just weird."

"Or part of a cult."

He cut a disbelieving look in her direction. "Let's talk with the drivers before we draw any concrete conclusions."

She wasn't sure she was off the mark, though. "I don't think Brantley Lourdes leads Public Exposure like a religious cult. But these people all listen to their leader as if nothing he says is wrong. Why else would two people be willing to crash into us, risking their lives?"

"You think Lourdes is capable of an attack?"

"I…I'm not sure." She had no facts to back up her feeling. But just like yesterday, she knew they were being watched. The unmistakable itch raised the hair on the back of her neck.

Heath grabbed her elbow, gently pulling her to a stop. He searched her eyes like he had a thousand times before. "You are sure." He tapped one-handed on his phone, putting it on speaker. "Jack, I'm not sure what's going on here. Stay sharp."

"Hang on, I'm still two blocks away. Don't do anything until I get there," Jack said.

"Man, we've moved past the corner. If I were Wade, I'd say I have a bad feeling about this. Hell, we're heading back to the SUV." Heath hung up.

"Hang on—" She wanted to delay the retreat, but one worried glance from her husband substantiated the uneasiness racing through her blood.

"We both know something around here isn't right, Kendall. How much digging have you done into this Public Exposure group? What's not in the file?"

She faced toward the SUV and began slowly moving down the sidewalk. It was no surprise that Heath took his steps backward next to her, keeping a wary watch behind them.

"Not enough apparently." But that was something she'd correct first thing she could.

"My general research last night gave me the impression they're mostly considered a do-good organization that encourages people to get off social media and interact with others."

Kendall couldn't shake the strange, creepy feeling. Even nature seemed to be in on setting the mood. No dogs barked, no birds chirped. The air hung heavy and thick.

"Excuse me. Can I help you?" A man stood in one of the orange doorways of the corner house.

Heath whipped around, ready for an attack. "Texas Ranger Heath Murray, sir. Sorry if we've alarmed you. Everything's fine."

Heath stopped moving toward the vehicle and didn't remove his fingers from his weapon. The thumb strap was unsnapped, ready to pull.

That creepy feeling got stronger, even though the man looked normal enough and splayed his empty hands for them to see.

"We'd appreciate if you returned indoors, sir." Kendall issued the directive, but the man stayed put. She couldn't force herself to move away.

"I'd rather know what's going on." He put his hands on his hips. "I'm calling the police."

Even though he didn't have a threatening posture, the situation felt off. Everything about it shouted a scenario from training. One where she turned her back and got a rubber bullet bouncing off of it.

"That's your right. Please go inside to make the call."

"I have my phone right here."

"Don't do it. Keep your hands in the air. I'm FBI. Do *not* reach for anything." She drew her weapon keeping the barrel toward the ground, then tapped Heath's shoulder, letting him know she had his back. "My partner is going to approach and verify that you're unarmed."

He was closer, so it was natural for him to check the man out.

"Okay, okay. I'll go back inside."

"You'll stay where you are," Heath shouted. "Keep your hands above your head, turn around slowly then take a step backward."

The man seemed innocent enough, but the uneasy feeling of the neighborhood persisted.

"There's a step. I'll fall." The man stretched his hands higher and took a step inside his open door.

"Stop!" they both shouted.

Heath moved toward the man, who finally froze. A little way down the street, she saw movement—two people running then ducking behind a car. One had hesitated when they'd shouted.

"Movement at nine o'clock," she informed Heath. "It might be our couple."

"One thing at a time. Jack will be here any minute." He took a final step, reaching the man, giving him instructions and letting him know what was coming next in the pat-down.

The neighborhood was still unusually quiet. Out of the corner of her eye she caught a glimpse of a car, heard the doors shut—no matter how quietly they tried to accomplish it. Every sound seemed to echo under the dense trees.

The man now faced her. Heath had explained how

he'd watched the glances of the two suspects the day before. From behind her sunglasses, she watched the man who'd gained their attention. Every so often he darted his gaze in the direction of where the people had been running.

Then a crazy gleam was in his eye and the corner of his mouth twitched—just like a person about to smile. He blinked heavily and stretched his eyebrows to relax his eyes before he noticed that she watched.

There it was again—his eyes darted quickly in the direction of a car starting.

"Heath, he's a distraction. Our couple is in a car down the street."

"You sure?"

"Ninety percent."

Heath removed handcuffs from his back pocket, locked one around the man's wrist. He quickly moved him next to the porch post and locked his other wrist around it. The man couldn't run away.

"Let's go." He turned and took off in one motion, getting several feet ahead of her.

They didn't bother keeping to the sidewalk, but simply ran across the lawns to the end of the block. A horn blared from behind, then next to them. *Jack.*

"Where are we running to? Hi, Kendall," Jack casually said through his open window.

A car peeled out, passing Jack's big truck and heading in the opposite direction.

"Go with Jack. Follow the car."

It wasn't her first rodeo. She'd been in charge before. She should be telling the guys what to do. But Heath took off around a parked car and she jumped

inside the truck. Maybe her husband had seen something she'd missed, since he wasn't heading in the direction of the car.

"What did this guy do?" Jack asked, quickly following the car down the next left.

She had one eye on the sedan and kept looking
around for anything suspicious. Again, there was nothing there, just the spine-chilling feeling that they were
being watched. Even while speeding down the street.

"Nothing solid. Yet."

HEATH DIDN'T HAVE time to explain why he ran in the opposite direction of the car. He'd seen the woman's pink
sweater in the thick shrubbery bordering the apartment
complex they were next to. At least he thought he'd seen
a pink sweater. Replaying the car's hasty exit in his
head, he couldn't visualize two people inside.

Only one.

So he'd taken off. Playing out a hunch.

Hell, he didn't know for certain if he chased the
woman from yesterday. How should he know if she
dressed in pink every day? What had caught his eye
might actually be another decoy. He had no way of
knowing. But the sweater happened to be the same color
as the car from the day before.

And he didn't believe in coincidences.

He headed to the north side of the house, where he'd
seen the top of a blond head before it ducked behind a
large oak tree. *Gotcha!*

Grabbing a decorative post to keep his feet under
him as he made a sharp right-angled turn, he followed
the fluff of pink between two houses. His jacket caught

on thorns as he barreled through the narrow path that was basically the width of his shoulders.

As a bead of sweat rolled into his eye, he twisted sideways, wishing to ditch the regulation jacket and hat. He used the sleeve to wipe his face when he slowed at the southwest corner of an old wooden home.

Dang. Rosebushes.

The woman was a lot slimmer than he was to have made it through this gauntlet without getting stuck. The thorny growth on the lattice at his shoulder might appear pretty from the street, but it kept him from scooting next to the house for cover.

Basically, he was sticking his neck out and hoping for the best. He looked around, then pulled back to a position that hid him from the street.

Slowing his breathing, he listened. He kept his movements small and again used his sleeve to wipe droplets of sweat from his face. He wasn't overheating. The humidity was high—like running through a rain cloud.

No matter how much he tried, he hadn't grown used to running in his suit. Boots, yes. Hat, yes. But suit, no. He'd run in boots and a hat his entire life. He'd always had a hat on his head. There weren't many pictures, going all the way back to before he could walk, without one.

And boots? Well, they were safer than tennis shoes where he'd grown up in Southwest Texas. Rattlers, scorpions and other varmints didn't like to be suddenly disturbed by a boy running after a horse or his father.

Funny what went through his head while chasing a subject.

Skylar Dawn on the other hand was dressed in all

sorts of frills. Boots were the exception not the rule—except on weekends at the Thompson's ranch.

He missed being with her every day, helping her pick out clothes—frilly girl or cowgirl. He wanted to sit beside her bed to read, then turn out the light with a goodnight kiss. Wanting to have memories with her, but also of him. Just like he did of his dad.

If things between him and Kendall stayed good today, maybe they'd get a chance to talk about him moving back in.

Chapter Nine

Kendall pulled her phone from her pocket, ready to report what had just happened. Three streets from the original neighborhood, Jack still followed at a distance far enough back not to call obvious attention. At this time of the morning, cars and trucks flooded this part of Dallas. And they basically all looked the same.

Their one saving grace was that Jack's vehicle hadn't been on the street very long. Hopefully, no one had seen her jump inside.

"What did the guy on the porch do?" Jack asked, tires squealing as he turned a sharp corner.

"He was the distraction."

"For the guy who hasn't done anything? That's sort of— Hang on."

She grabbed the handle above the door as Jack followed the path of the car, cutting across two lanes and pulling a U-turn. The bulkier truck required some of the sidewalk.

"I thought you had that light pole for sure." She tried to joke, but her heart raced, causing her voice to shake a little.

The man they followed turned again. Jack hit his

brakes, waiting two heartbeats before turning after him, but the sedan was already turning again.

"This guy is acting like he's being followed. Either he's paranoid or his aim is to make us paranoid. I can't tell." Jack securely gripped the wheel and made another U-turn. "I bet he's doubling back. I can get there before him. We'll already be on the street and he won't know we're in position."

"Good idea." She wished she'd thought of it. She wished she could think about anything useful. Her mind kept jumping between Skylar Dawn and Heath.

Focus was definitely necessary.

Truth was, she hadn't been in pursuit of a vehicle in a while. She was out of practice. Most of her work now happened behind a desk or in a lecture hall. Sure, she completed field interviews from time to time, but that wasn't the norm. At least not for her.

Then the file on Public Exposure had landed in her lap. Mysteriously after it had been closed for lack of evidence. She hadn't been able to tell if Jerry had supported her work or not.

"There he is." She pointed to the second car in the left turn lane. "Your hunch paid off."

"This would be easier if we had some backup and could leapfrog tailing him. Anyone around Harry Hines?"

"It wouldn't help. I couldn't catch the license plate number to call it in. Did you?"

"No. It's obscured by the other vehicle. Looks like it's just us for now."

The car passed them on the left with a car between them. Kendall pressed the video button on her phone without physically turning to look in his direction. Definitely their man, and he had no clue they were following him.

Or had been following him. They went straight as he slowed to turn. The sedan waited its turn in the feeder lane for the interstate. Just her luck.

"We're in the wrong lane."

"I got this." Jack jumped the short curb of the median and pulled a U-turn without slowing traffic. "Maybe you should call this in before it gets real."

As Jack sped up to catch her non-perpetrator, Kendall gripped the dashboard, knowing that his definition of *real* perfectly matched her husband's. All she could do was hope it wasn't real yet for Heath.

HEATH TUGGED HIS slacks higher onto his thighs and knelt, without touching the stone path or garden dirt. He could manage the balancing act for a few minutes. He pulled a blade of grass an edger had missed and almost tucked it between his teeth but thought again.

Kendall wouldn't have let Skylar Dawn mimic his actions. No telling what pesticides might be lingering around. This time he sort of believed there was something in the water. This street was as strangely quiet as the first one everyone had run from.

No dogs barked.

No cars drove past.

Nothing to disturb the heaviness in the air.

Humidity churned with the gut feeling that there was a lot more to Kendall's case than she was letting on. If she ever admitted to acting on her instincts, he might actually get the whole story.

Eventually.

If he earned her trust—no, *when* she trusted him again. He could wait for her. Just like he waited for the woman in the pink sweater to feel confident enough to leave wherever she was hiding.

Two houses with orange trim were nearby. He waited. His gray suit mixed in with the red roses, and he hoped his white Stetson lost its shape against the white house.

Waiting was the only option until Kendall returned. She might have called for backup, but he wouldn't know what type of car to look for. He'd turned his phone to silent, so it wouldn't even vibrate, just after tucking himself amidst the roses.

He wasn't making the mistake of his phone giving him away after the five or six thorns he'd fought.

Waiting was his specialty. But he had little choice in the matter. It wasn't like he had cause to go house-to-house looking for a woman he wasn't certain had even been there. What was he supposed to ask? Is there a pink sweater inside?

At least Kendall and Jack were on the trail of a sure thing. Jack was good. Kendall was better. They'd make sure the driver from yesterday didn't get away.

"WATCH OUT!" KENDALL braced herself between the middle console and the door. Her feet worked imaginary pedals. She stopped and accelerated the truck as if she were driving.

"Do you see him?" Jack asked.

"I hate the sun's reflection at this time of day. I can't see the lanes, let alone a gray sedan."

"Same here." Jack moved half of the truck onto the shoulder.

She finally had a better view and tugged at the seat belt to lean forward. "Wait. See the car darting half in the lane and back again?"

"Hang on."

As if she wasn't already.

She made the calls—one saying they were following a person of interest, then another to Jerry, the boss, who wasn't pleased they were darting through a major Dallas traffic artery during rush hour.

"Even one-sided, that conversation didn't sound good," Jack said when she hung up.

"We're not to put any lives in danger."

"Understood."

Jack drove with skill, taking advantage of a shoulder or exit lane—when there was one—to illegally pass without putting too many civilians at risk. But it didn't stop her heart from climbing into her throat.

"Looks like he's heading east. Maybe I-30 or south to I-45. What do you want to do?" he asked.

"Do you think he knows we're following?"

"Can't tell." Even behind his mirrored shades, Jack's eyes reflected his excitement. "Right now, he's not showing signs that he knows. He just seems in a hurry to get somewhere. If he heads into downtown proper, we're going to have a problem keeping our cover."

"And if he stays on either highway, we can coordinate a safe stop with Dallas PD."

"Looks like it's the Cadiz Street exit. You've got your direction. It's downtown. How aggressive do you want to get with this guy who hasn't really done anything?"

"When you put it like that…" So Heath hadn't mentioned to Jack that they'd nearly been killed the day before. Or that this guy had been involved. "Before he clearly fled, he was a person of interest. We only wanted a conversation."

With the man who tried to kill us.

"I'll get close enough for a clear look at the plates."

"I'll call it in, making all departments happy."

Jack got the truck just behind the sedan as it braked to exit. She snapped a picture of the plates and of the driver as they passed. Jack turned right at the light and the driver turned left. She made her calls.

The second one was to Jerry, who still wasn't happy.

"I've sent a unit to the address you gave me. No one's on the porch handcuffed or sipping their morning coffee. Did you get the name of this supposed subversive?" Jerry shouted.

"Ouch," Jack said softly.

The last thing she needed was one of Heath's partners cracking jokes. She shortened her breath, deliberately holding an exasperated sigh at bay. "There wasn't time."

"There are two agents cruising the area," her ex-partner said. "No sign of Murray either. Are you with him?"

"Looks like our guy is heading for the interstate. Should we follow or check on Heath?" Jack asked.

"Stay with the sedan," she told the Ranger. Into the phone she said, "Tell them not to shoot the man in the white hat."

FORTUNATELY, THERE WEREN'T any windows on this side of the house he leaned against.

Heath wanted to move but needed to stay put. Without anyone coming around, the woman in the pink sweater was bound to feel comfortable enough to come back outside. And most likely, she'd be heading down this path back to her place on the other street.

And he'd be there. Easy-peasy, as Skylar Dawn would say.

Unless the rosebush that he'd pretty much flattened caught on his jacket and kept him from moving. Then again, it might be his stiff legs that kept him from chasing someone down. He pushed the brim of his Stetson up with his forefinger, then wiped the sweat into his hairline.

Kendall had shaken her head at that habit more than once. It's why he tied a kerchief around his neck when he worked outside. His straw work hats had more ventilation than the regulation white beaver-felt Stetson. He wouldn't take a chance at drawing attention to himself by digging his sweat rag out of his inside pocket.

Still…he loved wearing the big hat. He loved being a Texas Ranger and all it stood for. Sweat ran down his back. Okay, the suit jacket he could live without.

A door opened.

It had to be close. Maybe even the front door to the building he leaned against. Light steps across the concrete porch headed in his direction. Heath pressed his shoulders closer to the wall and tipped his head back until his hat raised off his forehead.

"I'm sure they're gone now, Rita. Thanks so much for the lemonade. Oh my goodness. I don't need to wear this sweater until I'm back indoors. It's getting warm out here."

"You take care. I really enjoyed the visit. I just need

one more hug. It's going to be a while before I see you again."

There were two female voices. No distinguishable accents. Then additional steps—heels this time. An outer door gently swung shut.

"You guys take care on your trip," the woman who apparently lived there said. "Let us know when you get to Del Rio. That's quite a drive."

"Sure thing. I can't wait until you'll be there, too. Bye now."

More steps. Two doors shut. Humming.

It must be his lucky day.

The blonde he'd been chasing waltzed around the corner of the porch as she swung the pink sweater over her shoulder. She looked toward the street just as she passed him, missing that he stood in the rosebush.

"Howdy," he said with his best twang. He latched onto her elbow so she couldn't run. Then as she twisted to free herself, he said, "Don't do it."

Gone was the polite woman on the porch. She made a disgusted sound, stomped her foot and slung a couple of curse words in his direction.

"Who do you think you are? Let go of me."

He was surprised she didn't have a cell phone in hand, already trying to call for help. "Saundra Rosa?"

"How do you know my name? And what are you doing hiding in the rosebushes?"

"I had a couple of follow-up questions about yesterday."

That got her attention. "What about yesterday? I've never seen you before."

"That's right. I don't think we met at the accident.

Ranger Heath Murray, ma'am. We should probably move back to the sidewalk before someone calls the police." He gently and firmly moved the pink sweater lady in front of the house she'd been visiting.

"If I'm under arrest, aren't you going to read me my rights or something? I'd like to contact my lawyer before you cart me off to jail."

"Sure. Is that what you want…for me to arrest you? I was fine with a conversation."

"A conversation?" She looked truly bewildered.

"But if you want me to arrest you…" He reached for his handcuffs, forgetting they were on the wrists of a man almost two blocks away.

"No." She cleared her throat. "Not really. You just want to talk? What about?" She kept looking around, mainly up at the windows trimmed in orange.

Heath took a step sideways, blocking her view of the house behind him. "What were you doing in that part of Dallas?"

"I was delivering some items to a shelter." She stuck out her chin, defiantly, practically daring him to call her a liar.

"I promise this won't take but a minute. You told the officer yesterday that you were unfamiliar with the car you were driving. That's why you accelerated by mistake through the intersection."

"Yes. This is really about the car accident?" She lifted her hand and chewed on her short thumbnail.

"Is it your husband's?"

"What? No, I'm not married."

"Who did the car belong to?"

"Why does that matter? I'm paying for the damage to the other car. But I'm buying the Pink Thing. That's what my car reminds me of. You know, like the ice cream."

She popped a hip to one side and rested her hand there. It reminded him of when his daughter pretended she was a teapot. Saundra wasn't four years old. The pouting, put-out actions weren't reflecting well on a woman in her twenties either.

A couple of other doors had opened, including that of the home she'd been hiding inside. No one yelled or stepped onto their porch, but he got the feeling they weren't going away.

"That's good, very responsible." He brought his note-book out from his pocket. "This is actually for my office. More paperwork for the higher-ups."

"Are we done, then?" She pointed toward the unofficial path connecting to the next block. "I really have somewhere to be."

"Yeah, that just about covers it."

"Finally." She took steps back toward the house she'd left.

"One more thing." He pointed his finger in the air to stop her, then focused on her face, waiting on a reaction. "Why does Public Exposure want to kill my wife?"

Chapter Ten

By the time Jack took the right-hand turn and drove two blocks for the U-turn, the sedan and occupant were nowhere to be found. Kendall received a call that the Dallas PD hadn't seen the car driving down or near Cadiz Street.

"We heading back to Heath?" Jack asked.

"Yes. Hopefully he's had better luck."

She dialed, but knew by now her husband had probably silenced his phone. He was excellent about calling Skylar Dawn, like clockwork. But communicating with the rest of the world…well, he answered when it was convenient. She left a message and sent a text asking for his location and informed them they were ten minutes away.

"Thanks for your help with this, Jack. I won't be caught like this again."

"No problem. I've been helping Dallas PD out with a couple of cases until Wade is off desk duty." He was relaxed behind the wheel, taking morning traffic in stride now.

"I didn't realize Wade had been injured that badly."

"Well, it's his injuries combined with the fact that

he went against orders. Of course, I'm not complaining too loudly. I did get a girlfriend because of his misbehaving. Take a look in the console." He grinned, a charming smile that had been breaking hearts ever since she'd met him.

Wow, that had been six years ago. She raised the console lid, where a black jewelry box sat alone.

"Go ahead. Take a look. I'd like your reaction."

"My opinion won't mean much." She reached for it, shutting the console and sitting straight again, both excited and embarrassed at the same time.

"You're a woman, aren't you?" Jack laughed and switched lanes on the interstate. "And this is bling."

She flipped open the ring box. "Oh my, that's a lot of bling."

"I was hoping you'd react that way. I'm a little nervous. Okay, I admit it. I'm a lot nervous." He exited Oak Lawn, very close to the neighborhood where they'd left Heath.

"This is the woman you met last fall?"

"Yeah, Megan Harper. Honestly, I don't know what she's going to say. I mean, I think she'll say yes. It's the logistics of Austin versus Dallas. Who moves, that type of thing."

"No doubts about if she loves you?"

He shook his head. "There's been a zing there since the first time I held her in my arms."

Kendall didn't have any words. The ring was beautiful and she stared at it, missing the ring that normally sat on her fourth finger. She'd removed it and stuck it in her jacket pocket when she'd seen Heath on the stoop of Mrs. Pelzel's house the day before. Things had been hectic and she'd forgotten about it.

"It's gorgeous, Jack. I think she'll be very pleased. When are you going to ask her?"

"Soon. At least I hope to. Her parents are coming from England in a couple of weeks. I think I'll do the whole old-fashioned thing about asking her dad for permission."

The sweet gesture of respect was enough to bring tears to her eyes. It brought back many memories of her and Heath. She quickly closed the lid and stowed them away again.

"I didn't mean to…" Jack let the words trail off. He didn't have to say exactly what he meant. "You're really the only woman I could trust with this. My sister wouldn't be able to keep the secret. And there's no way I want my mom knowing before the ring's on Megan's finger. She'll have the whole wedding planned out without asking either of us for our opinions on anything."

Kendall laughed and dabbed at her eyes. "I know exactly what you mean. Mom had the country club booked in less than two hours. I remember telling Heath that she'd settle down. It never happened."

"I'm afraid that's what my mom's going to be like."

"Of course, I was busy with work, so I didn't really mind. I think Heath was more disappointed that I didn't help choose the cake flavors. The man does love cake."

"I've seen him chow down at office birthday parties."

They were at a stop light, and the truck filled with an awkward silence. Jack tapped his fingers on the steering wheel. Kendall flipped her phone over, checking for messages.

Nothing.

Heath could take care of himself. But in this crazy world, she'd prefer to have his back. Or to know that someone did, at least.

"This is the longest red light ever. Don't you have lights?"

Without a word, Jack flipped a switch and a siren sounded. Cars slowed at the busy intersection long enough for them to get across.

"If he was in trouble, you would have heard from him."

"I'm sure you're right. It's just…"

"It's okay, Kendall. I get it. I remember how I freaked not knowing if Megan was okay." He pressed his lips together and shifted in his seat.

The subject made him just as uncomfortable as it did her. She wanted to believe that Heath was okay. The belief somehow made her feel more professional. And no matter what she'd said yesterday when she'd first seen him, they weren't just professionals. They were married.

No matter their differences, he'd always be the father of her child. She'd never want any harm to come to him. Period.

They were still a couple of blocks away, and Jack was driving as fast as traffic would allow. The lights and sirens were off. He'd only used them to get through the intersection. So she did what she and Heath needed to do more of. She started talking.

"You'll have to tell me what Megan's like. Oh, and when are you going to ask her? Does anyone else know? I don't want to spill your secret."

"She'll be up this weekend. We could all have dinner if you want," he said before wincing a little. "It doesn't have to be with Heath."

"It's Heath's weekend with Skylar Dawn." As if that was a real answer. She took a deep breath, deciding to be honest. "I know this is awkward. The one good thing about working together for a while will mean we actually have time to talk. We've both been avoiding it."

"That's a good plan." He pointed to her car. "See, he's okay."

He was right. Heath leaned against the brick wall of a 7-Eleven convenience store, as casually as a real cowboy leaned against anything. She was relieved and furious all at once. Thank God he was okay, but why hadn't he returned her calls?

Jack stopped and she quickly jumped from his truck. "Thanks for the help, and I'll see you soon. There's no need for you to stick around and witness me murdering my husband."

HEATH LOOKED UP from under his hat. He had spotted Jack's truck midway up the block and slid his phone back inside his pocket. He had four texts and a message that he hadn't had time to listen to, but he knew what it contained.

Kendall would be—there wasn't another word for it—worried.

"I guess you didn't catch your guy?" He stood straight, stopping himself from walking to her.

"Well, it looks like you didn't catch yours either." Her voice was controlled and deliberate.

He recognized the compressed lips, the restraints

she held on herself. He'd been on the receiving end of the cool wait-until-we're-alone look a few times. She pulled the keys from her pocket, spinning the key ring around her finger and heading for the SUV.

"Um…Kendall. Wait. We're not—" He reached to stop her, but not before Saundra stepped through the front doors of the building with a cup of coffee.

"Holy cow. That's—" She pivoted, doing an about-face toward him and grabbed his arm, taking them to the corner of the building. "What the heck's going on?"

"I was trying to tell you. Saundra ran into me and, after a couple of minutes, she decided to explain something to us about yesterday's accident."

"Oh, that's such a relief."

Dammit. Her go-to phrase let him know that she was more than a little ticked off at him. But at least the words she said loud enough for Saundra to hear were cloaked in a syrupy, concerned tone.

One surprised look and Special Agent Kendall Barlow was back in charge and had herself under control. "Miss Rosa. What would you like to explain? Wait. Should we try to find some place that's a bit more quiet? Is there a coffee shop nearby?"

"I only have a minute. I've explained to Heath that this is all just a big mistake and I need to get to work. I don't really know Bryan Marrone. I mean, I've seen him driving down the street, but that's it. I don't *know* him. You see?"

"Do you want to take her in for questioning?" he asked, crossing his arms, determined to keep a straight face.

"You have to believe me," Saundra pleaded. "I didn't really *do* anything except let him crash into my car."

There shouldn't be anything funny in Saundra's explanation. She didn't know him, but she'd let him crash into her car? He'd heard a lot of explanations over the years—every Texas highway patrolman did. Hers just made his top-ten list. There was hilarious, and then just plain absurd.

"Miss Rosa, I think we'd be better off having this discussion somewhere other than the 7-Eleven parking lot." Kendall gestured toward a couple of men walking inside the store.

"Oh, no. I couldn't possibly go to the FBI building. That's totally out of the question."

"Miss Rosa, please." Kendall opened her arms. One slowly moving behind Saundra and one gesturing more toward him on the corner. "Let's at least get away from the door."

She moved. Kendall moved. He kept his back to the ice machine and glanced around every other minute, making sure no onlooker stared too closely.

"You don't really think I tried to kill you. Do you? I mean, no one was really hurt." Saundra sipped her coffee, stretching her eyes open as large as they could get.

Kendall coughed or choked like she'd swallowed wrong. Heath tried not to look at the varying shades of pink powder on Saundra's eyelids. But damn, she was serious. She really didn't think she'd done anything wrong.

If he'd had a second set of handcuffs, she wouldn't be walking around drinking the coffee he'd bought. This was the very reason they needed backup, or that Bureau-issued sedan. If they'd had it, he would have arrested Saundra Rosa at the rosebushes.

Did Kendall feel the same way, or did she want to tackle the investigation from a different angle? Standing slightly behind her, he couldn't see her face and couldn't make a judgment call on what she thought.

"Thank you for your honesty, Miss Rosa. Did Ranger Murray get your contact information?" Kendall paused while Saundra nodded. "We'll be in touch."

"Hey, Saundra. You'll be needing these." He returned her cell and ID he'd held onto during their conversation and walk.

"Oh, right. Thanks for not arresting me, Heath." Saundra power walked away from them, retracing the steps they'd taken earlier down the Wycliff Avenue sidewalk. Then she slowed, bending her head over her cell.

"I'd really like to know who she's texting right now."

"What in the world were you thinking?" Kendall turned on him as soon as Saundra was out of sight.

"What?" He honestly didn't know which way the conversation would go from here.

"You couldn't give me a heads-up that you'd not only caught your suspect, but that she was getting coffee?" Kendall vehemently pointed toward the 7-Eleven door while walking toward the SUV.

The key ring was still slipped over her finger. She clicked the unlock button and moved toward it, as if she'd suddenly remembered that she had a car. They didn't need to argue out in the open next to the trash.

Whatever reprieve he'd received from her being upset was apparently gone as they sat in the front seat. She kept twirling her keys instead of using them. She leaned forward, dropping her head on the steering wheel and taking deep breaths.

His hand lifted to drop on her back. After a moment's hesitation, he let it. She didn't shrug it off.

"I was calling you when I saw Jack's truck halfway up the block."

Kendall puffed her cheeks and blew the air out with a slow *wuff*. As much as he wanted to continue to touch her, he raised his hand and rested it on the seat-back. She turned the key, cranked the AC to high and pointed the vents toward her face.

A lot of effort was going into her movements to keep herself calm. He knew her, knew what she did when she was too upset to speak politely. Blasting the AC in her face was just a substitute for fanning herself.

"Why don't you just go ahead and say whatever it is you're trying hard *not* to say? Or maybe we could go collect my handcuffs?"

"You know that the first man is no longer there?"

"Sure. I had to walk past the house with Saundra. Is that why you're sore?"

"Good grief. No. I was—" She put the SUV in gear. "Do you want to see if the man is still in the house?"

"You tell me. It's your case."

"Is that really how this is going to play out? You take off alone, darting through houses that seem to all be part of the same organization where—"

"Yeah? Where what? Did you expect them to ambush me?"

"It wouldn't be the first time. Would it?" Kendall visibly clenched her jaw.

"Are you really going there? I'd prefer to have one argument at a time."

"If it's relevant to this particular argument then I

think we—" Her cell rang and she clicked the button, connecting the hands-free. "Barlow."

"This is Special Agent in Charge Lou Grayson with the Portland office. Have I caught you at a convenient time?"

Kendall pulled into an alley separating Rawlins and Hall Streets. She took the phone off speaker quicker than his mare headed for the barn for dinner. She began to get out, but he stopped her. She could stay in the SUV while he collected his cuffs.

Heath hated to admit as he got out of the SUV that he had another bad feeling. If a Portland agent was calling about the case, Kendall wouldn't have needed privacy.

"Dammit," he muttered to himself. "What the hell is going on?"

Chapter Eleven

Kendall locked the SUV and followed thirty feet behind her husband.

"Special Agent Grayson, what can I do for the Portland agency?"

"Join us. And it's Lou. Please."

What?

His words stopped her in her tracks at the corner—a
good vantage point to have Heath's back if something
went wrong.

"I apologize, Lou, but now might be the wrong time.
I'm out in the field—"

"I'll text you my direct number."

Heath walked up the sidewalk to pick up his handcuffs.

She needed to get off the phone. "Special Agent
Grayson, I need three minutes. Sorry."

She tapped the red disconnect button and stashed the
phone in her pocket. The bright silver still hung around
the pole, locked in place. The neighborhood continued
to be abnormally quiet and vacant for a block in Uptown. It was just weird to be outside this long and not
hear a single bird or dog.

Heath was on the porch, key in hand, as he collected

his restraints. No surprises. He didn't knock on the door to see if the man was inside. He did everything she'd asked. Then he retraced his steps. No one left their home. No car drove by. Her husband was ten feet away and she ran back to the SUV, dialing while attempting to be as focused on her duty as possible.

"My apologies, Lou."

"Glad you called back," he said without any irritation in his voice. "I know this might seem like it's out of the blue, Kendall, but you come highly recommended."

"I'm very flattered and honored, sir. But I didn't apply for a transfer."

"Let me give you a better idea of why you were recommended."

Lou Grayson recounted some of the high points of her last evaluation. She heard the words, knowing they were true…but…why her? *Why now?* Those words kept ringing over and over in her mind while Heath turned the corner toward the SUV.

He stopped, took his own cell out and turned his back to her. All the signs were there that her husband suspected something was wrong.

How would she explain the phone call from Portland without lying to him? Her only two options were avoid or evade.

"Kendall? Are you still there?"

Tempting as it was to claim a bad connection and deal with this another time, she didn't move through life like that.

"Yes, sir. I think I'm still a little stunned."

"As I said, this might seem sudden to you, but we've actually been considering it for quite a while."

"May I ask how long, sir?"

"Since your partner was promoted. You'd be taking over our cybercrime unit, when the group leader retires in three months. Of course, we'd like you here well before then to learn the ropes."

"I'll need time to think about the move."

"How long do you think you need?"

"As long as you'll give me. This is a big change."

"I don't doubt it. How about a week?"

"Sure. Thank you, sir."

Heath stuck his cell in his pocket and placed both hands on his hips, clearly frustrated. She waved at him to return while she exchanged pleasantries with Grayson and disconnected.

"I called for a neighborhood patrol. They'll pick up Marrone when he comes home."

"*If* he comes home. He might be on his way to Mexico."

"More like Del Rio," he said.

"Where?" She couldn't have heard him right. "Del Rio, Texas?"

"Yeah. I overheard Saundra talking to a woman on Vandelia Street. I thought she was just making up the trip. You know, as an excuse. Then again, the woman said she'd love it there. As if she'd been before. Does it mean something?"

"Brantley Lourdes has land there. It's almost compound-like." Practically giddy, she grabbed Heath's arm, shaking it with excitement. "That's where Public Exposure's headquarters are."

"Did you issue a BOLO for Marrone?"

She shook her head, and Heath dialed the Rangers. She flipped open her notebook with the license plate of the sedan they'd been following. He gave them the information needed for the all-points bulletin.

Continuing to smile, she steered the SUV toward FBI headquarters.

She was excited. No. *Ecstatic.*

The couple that had tried to smash their car the previous day definitely worked for Public Exposure. She had a connection. Together they would break this case open. She was sure of it now.

"DPS will get him if he's on a highway out of town to Del Rio." Heath stashed his cell back in his pocket. "Do you want Dallas PD to pick up Saundra Rosa? It might be a good idea to see if she's willing to come to your office on her own. You might be able to flip her there before Public Exposure sends a lawyer."

"You mean *you* might be able to flip her. She seemed very eager to cooperate and kept looking to you when she answered. Sort of like you promised her something. Did you?"

"I've been told that women feel safer with a Texas cowboy around. I simply explained that we needed to file some reports."

"You said 'Yes ma'am, no ma'am.' And you told her we had to file reports. That made her stop what she was doing and let you buy her a cup of coffee while you waited to speak with me?"

Her husband cocked her head to the side and lifted a finger—a sure sign she wasn't going to like his next words.

"I might have asked her why she tried to kill my wife."

"And her response…?"

"Crying. Full-blown, mascara-running, fall-to-her-knees weeping. As a highway patrolman, I've seen a lot of women cry. I've told you some of the stories. But I've never seen anything like this, Kendall. She even asked me for forgiveness."

"And then she denied everything?"

"Absolutely everything. Even down to knowing Marrone, at least knowing him well. As she said, they wave at each other when they pass each other on the street."

"Do you believe her?"

"Hell, no."

"Thank goodness. For a minute there, I thought you'd totally lost it in the past six months." She pulled into the FBI parking lot. "That woman was lying through her teeth."

"Sadly true."

HEATH HATED THE idea of obtaining a visitor's badge and tagging behind Kendall as she went through her office. He'd been there, done that, and he'd felt like a puppy on a leash.

"I'll wait out here. Make some phone calls."

"You're sure? No coffee or anything else?" Kendall didn't wait long for an answer. She was already out of the SUV and walking fast. "I'll text when I'm coming down. It may be a little while."

"No problem."

Heath didn't want to draw the attention of FBI security. He had other things to think about instead of justifying why he was waiting. He kept the door open and his feet on the parking lot asphalt when all he wanted was to move and get rid of some nervous energy.

His phone began vibrating. "That was fast," he said in answer.

"Hey, Heath. Just letting you know, man. The house you wanted us to surveil has already had four visitors. I texted the pictures. No car fitting the description or plate number you issued the BOLO for."

"I owe you one, Jason."

"Not for long. My daughter wants riding lessons. When she mentioned lessons, I actually told my wife I knew a real cowboy. Me and my big mouth."

"Anytime. We can ride a couple of times and let her see if it's something she really wants."

"That would be terrific. How long you want me to hang around Rosa's house?"

Heath scrolled through the pictures—three men in dress shirts and ties, one woman. "I think we've got a start here. Thanks again."

"I'll talk to my wife and we'll make a date," Jason said.

"You've got my number."

"Let's go with a heavy patrol in the neighborhood."

Heath hung up and first texted, then called Wade at the office.

"What's up?"

"I'm at the FBI headquarters waiting on Kendall to get a Bureau-issued car."

"Thanks for checking in?" Wade asked it as a question, probably since that wasn't the normal routine. "Okay, what do you want me to do with the pictures you texted? I assume they're surveillance photos."

"You got it. I'm wondering if one of the men is Brantley Lourdes."

"Man, all you had to do was open your smartphone for that answer. He's a pretty well-known guy. But I'll run the other faces for you. While I let the program kick this around, how's it working out with Kendall?"

"It was a rocky start. Then I thought I'd done something good. Now we're back to barely speaking." Enough personal business. "Check if the others have ties to Public Exposure."

"You got it," he said, clicking keys on his computer. "You two are all over the place. Why don't you just tell her you want to move back home?"

"It's not that simple."

"Sure it is."

"It's not like I haven't tried, man."

"For a married man, you sure don't know anything about women."

"And you do? I seem to recall that you're single and haven't had a date in—"

"Yeah. Got it. Minding my own love life. The people in your pictures are all board members for Public Exposure. I'll text you their names and pertinent info. They're from all over the country."

"Question is…why are they all in Dallas? And why are they all visiting a home of a suspect?"

"Good question. When do you intend to find out?"

"Soon. See you, man." Heath hung up.

A horn honked behind him. Kendall had kept her word to be fast.

Just tell her you want to move back home.

The thought was there. The courage…not so much. He was afraid she'd tell him why it wouldn't work.

Instead, he stayed focused on their investigation.

"A buddy of mine at DPD is watching Saundra Rosa's place."

"Already?" she asked.

"I had some time while you were on your call. Anyway, he grabbed a couple of pictures of visitors, and I sent them to Wade. One was Brantley Lourdes."

"We only spoke to her an hour ago and he's already making a house call?" She pulled out from the parking lot.

"It gets better. Seems most of his board of directors for Public Exposure is here in town." He tapped a knuckle against the window, giving her time to think.

"You know I'm not someone to play hunches. I like good old-fashioned investigating and facts. But every feeling I have tells me that company is dirty."

They'd played this scenario before, back when they first worked together. His hunches had proved him right after a bet that it couldn't be that simple. That bet had gotten him the first date with the love of his life.

He didn't do a lot of dwelling in the past, but working with Kendall was a constant reminder that he'd been in love from the first time he'd laid eyes on her. She'd been a rookie agent working one of her first cases and he'd been her backup at several remote locations. A little town south of Burleson serving warrants and looking for a handgun.

Following one of his hunches about the gun's location led to their first date. Yeah, he'd won the bet that afternoon and they'd both won that weekend.

"Heath? Yo, Heath!" She snapped her fingers in front of his face. "Did you have nice trip? Ready to get back to work? So…if they're all here in town, it looks like whatever's going down will likely be soon."

"We'll need a warrant," she said.

"It'll be easier to get it through my department. You have a longer chain of command than I do."

"If I could just get my hands on some hard evidence that this is a cybercrime, they'd give me a lot more resources and a little more leeway."

"Good thing you know someone who has a little leeway then," he answered.

"You know, since we're working together, I don't mind you staying at the house."

That was sort of out of the blue. But he liked it. Riding to and from work, having dinner together… *Wait.*

"I don't want to put you out. I mean, it's only convenient if you don't stay at your mom's."

"True. I… I think it's a good idea. Especially after how upset Skylar Dawn was last night."

Did she want him to stay at the house to work things out? Or was it because their daughter was upset?

Did it really matter? Did he care why he would be waking up with his girls?

Nope.

"Sounds good. I'll even cook."

THE BOLO ON Marrone paid off. Texas Highway Patrol spotted the car and picked him up south of Waco. He could be transported back to Dallas County Jail soon after she made a request. They could interview him while he awaited a hearing for his parole violation. Again, Kendall owed Heath for arranging the BOLO.

If she hadn't been working the case for more than six months, she might begin to get an inferiority complex.

Late Tuesday afternoon, they easily procured the warrant. Hearing that their suspect had fled the city and had an outstanding violation, the Waco judge had no objections regarding extradition. They could collect it in the morning and question their suspect upon his return.

"I still don't understand why the Public Exposure board of directors met here in Dallas. It isn't the main headquarters, and none of them actually live here."

"It may just be a coincidence," Heath said.

"You've never believed in a coincidence in your life. I don't know how many times you've told me that."

"True. You want to take the munchkin out for chicken strips or pick up food on the way home?"

She smiled. This was the normal routine when it was her husband's turn to cook anything except breakfast. "I think she'd prefer to have you at home all to herself. I'll make myself scarce."

Was that a look of disappointment that he hid by rubbing his face with his hand?

A real look or one she projected onto him? She couldn't let sentiment or wishful thinking get in the way of the case.

"You seem to be thinking pretty hard, Agent Barlow. If you're trying to tell me that my cooking's not so good. Don't worry. No illusions there."

"I wasn't thinking that even if it is true. Would you mind dropping me at the house? I'll send mom home while you take Skylar Dawn to dinner. She'll get a kick out of that."

Kendall turned the SUV onto their street.

"You got it." His agreement sounded like a forced confession.

"You don't have to sound so thrilled about it."

"Not a problem I get it."

"I don't think you do." She parked in the driveway and he practically jumped out of the car faster than stepping away from a bucking bronc. "Wait…"

But he didn't hear her. And she didn't chase him. Instead she sent her daughter skipping to a fast food dinner and her mother home for the night before she could complain too loudly about it.

Then she took advantage of an hour to herself, poured too much bubble bath into the tub and soaked until the water grew cold.

Wrapping herself in her comfy robe, she promised herself the nap would only last a couple of minutes when her head hit the pillow.

And not one time did she think of a way out. She couldn't practice the right thing to say. Whatever was needed to be said to Heath—her husband and her partner on this crazy journey.

Chapter Twelve

The third day working with Heath began with him in their kitchen if the wonderful smells in the house meant anything. Kendall had never been a night owl. She'd always thought of herself as a morning person. Morning workout or run, coffee and a quick shower had always been her style. Then she'd met a man who fed livestock at the crack of dawn every day and made fun of how late she slept.

This morning she could barely roll over. She'd experienced a total lack of sleep from tossing and turning. The awesome dreams of Heath seemed short-lived, and she struggled to get back to that place where everything was happy…and perfect.

The smell of coffee and biscuits finally had her stretching across the twisted sheets and eager to find her travel mug. Her mother didn't drink coffee. Just tea—morning, noon and night.

Coffee. Coffee. Coffee. The smell beckoned her to get out of bed.

Oh, God. I slept all night.

Shoving the sheets aside, she pulled on running shorts and a sports bra. She needed a couple of miles to work out the kinks and get her blood pumping. But she could start with one of those fresh-baked biscuits—and coffee.

"Hey, good morning." She came around the corner, expecting Heath and Skylar Dawn. Taken off guard, she smiled at her mother setting a plate of food at the bar.

"I told him you don't eat like this in the morning, but he insisted."

"Morning, Mother. Don't take this the wrong way, but why are you here this early?"

"Heath called and asked me to come and take Skylar Dawn to school."

"I can handle that."

"I told him as much, but again, he insisted. He said to check your phone and that you didn't have time for any exercise. He also left you this smelly stuff." She pointed to a pot of coffee.

My hero. Heath had found their coffeemaker from wherever her mother had hidden it. After moving it to the back of the pantry, her mother had bought a single-cup coffeemaker for the counter. It was the perfect temperature for a cup of flavored tea without any mess or boiling teapots.

"Where's Skylar Dawn?" She poured the brewed java into a mug and blew across the top.

"In the tub. In fact, I need to check on her."

"Mother, I'm sure Heath gave her a bath last night," she said a little louder, to carry down the hall where her mom was already headed.

"She fed horses this morning and stepped in some—oh good Lord, you know what she stepped in out there. You should listen to your messages, darling. I'm not sure it's really time sensitive, but he said it was about your case."

Kendall laughed on her way back to the bedroom and her phone. She was fairly certain that if—and that was a big if—her daughter had stepped in you-know-what, Heath had cleaned her up. But her mother was her mother.

Another bath wouldn't hurt Skylar Dawn. She'd play in the bubbles and smell like pink bubblegum at day care. No harm done.

She checked her messages. "Another agency—yours—served a warrant on Marrone's rental house. They found Saundra Rosa's body. Don't forget to pick up a Bureau sedan. Meet you there."

When Heath mentioned "body," she scalded her tongue, forgetting the coffee was still hot. She hurriedly dressed, pulling her hair into a ponytail. She scooped her creds, keys and phone into a pocket. Opened her gun safe and holstered her weapon.

"Gotta run, sweet girl." She blew an air kiss to Skylar Dawn. "Thanks for taking her this morning."

"I guess his message was important after all."

"Very." The door shut behind her as she ran to the SUV. *Dang it. I forgot my coffee.*

HEATH CHECKED HIS WATCH. "Special Agent Barlow is a few minutes away," he told the medical examiner, not really knowing how long it would take.

"I've got a couple of minutes. I know you want her to see the scene, but once transport arrives, I'll have to move the victim."

"I understand."

He kept taking pictures. Every angle possible from where he'd been allowed. Then more of each room he could see.

"It looks like she came for a visit and Marrone dosed her with something. We found a needle mark on her left arm." Supervisory Special Agent Jerry Fisher had mentioned his theory several times to anyone who would listen.

Too many times. An uncomfortable number of times.

There was one problem with his theory. Bryan Marrone hadn't returned to his house. Picked up south of Waco, he was dressed the same as he'd been the previous morning and in the same car. Jerry didn't know that the Dallas PD had been sitting on this house until the BOLO for Marrone had been canceled.

Absolutely a setup.

Yeah, that bad feeling had returned.

Heath kept avoiding direct conversation with Kendall's supervisor. Besides the fact that he just didn't care for his wife's former partner, he didn't want to give the agent an opportunity to tell him his services were no longer needed.

The two players they had connected to Public Exposure were accounted for. One dead—honestly, he was sorry for that. Maybe if he hadn't spoken to her or bought her a cup of coffee… It sounded heartless, but he hadn't killed her. The only justice he could give was to find her killer.

And it sure as hell wasn't Bryan Marrone.

He left the house with orange trim and saw Kendall walking through the police and onlookers, credentials in hand, "FBI" coming repeatedly from her lips.

"Morning. Glad you could make it," he greeted her without saying what he really wanted to say. Okay putting that into words right here wouldn't have worked. But a guy could think about it.

"Any theories as to how she was killed?" she asked, continuing her power walk up the sidewalk.

"Plenty. I'll let you decide for yourself." He stayed put. No reason to crowd the small house with one more body.

She turned, taking a backward step. "Did Skylar Dawn really step in you-know-what?"

He laughed and nodded. "I bet your mother had her in the bath faster than the wicked witch melted."

He stared after his wife, liking the way she flashed her creds at the other staring officers. There had been plenty of times after they were first married that he'd watched men looking at her and simply pointed to his wedding ring. She was definitely a beautiful, confident woman worth admiring.

Returning to his phone, he looked carefully at the body of a totally different type of woman. A young woman who loved pink and had unaccounted-for visitors yesterday.

"Why did you run, Bryan Marrone?" he asked under his breath. "Who were you afraid of?"

"Who's afraid of whom?" Kendall asked, coming to stand next to him. She tipped her head slightly to look at him before blocking her eyes with her sunglasses. "Oh. Well, Jerry's wrong."

"Yep."

"Is anyone checking out her house?"

"Yep." He pointed to three houses down, where a do-not-cross tape had been hung.

"Darn." She snapped her fingers like she'd missed an opportunity. "I don't suppose…"

He nodded. "I took a look at it earlier. Everything looks comfortably messed up."

"'Comfortably messed up'?" she asked with a tweak of her head.

"Like someone looked for something but didn't want us to know they were in a hurry. No phone. No laptop. But the TV was still there." He handed her his phone.

"Oh. I suppose you got pictures?"

"Yep." He stepped aside for the gurney that would remove the body. "I have a different adventure for you."

"The pink car?" She looked at him above her glasses and smiled.

That was the super smart agent he'd fallen in love with—one step ahead of the rest. "It's probably nothing."

"But an adventure nonetheless." She winked. "My car or yours?"

"You drive. Swing by my truck for my laptop. I'll call Jason at DPD and find out where they towed the Pink Thing for repairs."

It took them a good hour to drive to the repair shop. That in itself raised a red flag.

"Why would someone who lived in Uptown have their car towed to McKinney? That's just not logical, unless you have family or someone's doing you a favor." Kendall pulled on gloves before she began looking through Saundra's car. "And Saundra didn't have family."

"No one who works here has seen or heard of our

victim. I didn't get the impression that any of them were lying. Did you?"

"No. Darn it. They seemed genuinely upset when you told them she'd been murdered."

"Um. I think that was because she owed them for the work they'd already started."

Kendall flipped the glovebox open. "Papers. Owner manual. Looks like she owned the car."

"She definitely liked pink." Heath continued to take pictures of sneakers, a sweater, T-shirts and running shorts, all in varying shades of pink.

Kendall leaned down to look under the passenger seat. "Candy wrappers, twenty-seven cents and an eraser."

"Eraser?"

"Yeah, it's Betty Boop. A fat Betty Boop, but I recognize the cartoon character." She set it on the seat cushion.

"Can I see that?" Heath asked after taking pictures.

Kendall handed it to him, and he pulled the head off to reveal a USB. "A flash drive?"

"*This* I can work with." He smiled from ear to ear.

"I bet they were looking for this at her place. Perhaps it's a connection to Public Exposure."

Heath took something from his jacket pocket and plugged it into his phone. Then he plugged the flash drive into it.

"I should probably warn you that we shouldn't look at the evidence yet." She waved at him to let her see the screen, too. "You're one of the only guys I know who carries a flash drive attachment for his phone."

"Hey, I resent that remark. I picked it up this morning from the ranch. This case is about computers." He shrugged. "Why wouldn't I?"

"That looks like a complicated encryption. Do you think you'll be able to break it?"

"Looks like it's going to be a tech thing after all. Yours or mine?" he asked.

"This time, I think I have to go with mine. They have a bigger department. If we connect Public Exposure to cybercrime, they'll put a rush on it. DC might get involved."

"Then our adventure would be over."

With the exception of one major thing—they needed a shred of proof for the big leagues to come on board. She didn't know why that was important to her. Maybe it was justification that she hadn't wasted six months of her time and taxpayer resources. Maybe it felt strange, and she wanted a solid explanation.

Or maybe she wanted a big break to boost her career. She couldn't tell. It was probably a little of all of the above.

"Maybe not yet. I'd like to flash this in front of Bryan Marrone to get his reaction."

"It's a long drive to Waco." He bagged their evidence.

"I asked Dallas PD to extradite him. He'll be here in the morning. Honestly, did you think I wouldn't?"

"Nope. Just hoping for more time with you. My couple of days is officially up." They spoke to others in the garage and waited on local law enforcement to take over the car.

"We make a pretty good team, Barlow." He touched the small of her back to guide her through the door first.

"That we do, Murray."

THE OFFICIAL CALL came that Heath would be continuing with the case. The city of Dallas wanted someone local representing their interests.

Avoidance. Who was worse? Him or Kendall? Both of them took the opportunity to talk with as many other people as possible. Right up to the time they were in the SUV and they went over their plan to interview Marrone.

"I like watching you work. I always have." Blocks away from the house…his mouth finally caught up to his heart.

"Right. We only worked one case together."

"Hey, I watched from home."

"Right."

That tone…one of disbelief. Normally it was a good reason to stop and walk away to avoid what would follow. Not today.

"Kendall, I need you to believe me that I don't want you to stop working. Wait a minute before you do the psychological profile and get angry."

"Okay."

"See, I probably did mean it six months ago. But I don't know why. My mom has worked every day of my life. If it wasn't for her, things around me would never have happened. I know you're capable of handling everything."

Seconds ticked by but she wasn't angry. The emotion would have shown up in her movements.

"Then why?"

"I was scared. For you. For Skylar Dawn. Don't get me wrong, I wanted another kid for the right reasons, but I wanted you around to protect all of us."

"Your dad?"

"Yeah," he squeaked the word out. "Things happen that are beyond our control. Dad is gone because he fell not because he chased criminals through the street."

"I wish you'd told me this earlier. Maybe…"

"It's hard for a man in my line of work to admit he's scared. Even though we know the risks."

They were in the driveway and in a good place. As much as he wanted to stay…she needed time.

"See you in the morning."

His wife waved from behind the wheel without looking at him. He didn't press for an answer just got in his truck. For the first time in months, he might get a good night's sleep.

Chapter Thirteen

KENDALL BEGAN HER questions from the door and slowly moved closer, taking a chair and inching it even closer to invade Marrone's space. Several people watched from the two-way mirror. It was a classic technique.

"Come on, Bryan. We understand if you're scared." Kendall was an excellent interrogator. She had the Reid technique down pat. She'd planned this one down to the minute, or cue. "I mean, they killed your friend. Who wouldn't be scared?"

After she moved in close, after she commiserated, then Heath would enter and say they found proof that Marrone was guilty. They'd discussed exactly what he was to do while returning from McKinney the day before— and again this morning.

"Bryan, you've got to give me something to work with."

"Are you sure Saundra's dead?" He gulped. The young man's Adam's apple moved up and down his thin neck.

"Yes, hon. I may be alone in thinking you're not guilty." She placed a hand on his knee. "None of my coworkers believe that you left town right after you saw us yesterday morning."

That was Heath's cue.

A light tap sounded on the door. He let himself in, and Kendall withdrew her hand with a guilty look.

"Special Agent Barlow, there's no reason to continue the questioning. The techs found this in Saundra Rosa's car. It proves that Marrone here is guilty. He has one, too."

Bryan might have been watching him toss the evidence bag onto the table, but both him and Kendall stared at the young man's reaction. Everything about his face screamed that he knew what was on the flash drive.

Then he relaxed. He sank down in the chair and acted like he couldn't have cared less what evidence they had. He knew. Whatever was on the flash drive, Marrone knew. It's what he'd been looking for in the apartment.

Kendall's tactics changed. She jumped up from her seat and grabbed the bag. "You know what this is, don't you?"

"You don't have anything on me 'cause you can't read that thing without the key. You'll never get the algorithm before we kick some ass around here."

"You'd rather go away for murder than tell us?"

"I'm innocent."

"Your fingerprints are on the syringe and once we—"

"No. They're not." He tried to bring his arms above his head, but the handcuffs jerked his hands back to the table. "I think I'd like my lawyer now."

They'd gotten nothing definitive. Kendall would be upset.

He wasn't. No one had called to tell him to remove himself from the investigation. That meant another day working with his wife.

Another day to work up the courage to tell her he wanted to come home.

"What do you say? Ready to go home?" Heath asked.

Not Kendall. She was ready to rework everything she had on Public Exposure. "What do you think he meant by 'before we kick some ass'?"

They left the county jail, changed cars and headed out. It was the first time she'd walked to the passenger door and let him drive their SUV home. But it was a silent ride while she scoured her notes, flipping page over page over page.

He didn't bring it to her attention that they'd arrived home. He grabbed his hat and made it to the steps before his daughter threw open the door.

"Daddy, make me fly." Skylar Dawn took a running start and leapt into his arms.

Heath had completely forgotten about his injured side. When she hit his ribs, a smoldering burn kicked into a bonfire of pain. He hid it as best as he could before he lifted his daughter into the air and spun her around like an airplane, complete with sputtering propeller noises.

It didn't last long.

"Hey, sweetie. Let me grab some jeans, then I can play in the backyard with you." Heath used his key and opened the front door.

"Skylar Dawn, come get your bunny and jacket," Kendall called from the car.

Maybe…just maybe she hadn't seen him. Either way, he needed a minute to catch his breath.

He rounded the corner, heading for his bedroom closet. He barely had his shirt unbuttoned and an old pair of jeans thrown on before his mother-in-law appeared in the doorway with laundry.

"Oh dear Lord. You scared me." The stack of clothes fell to the floor as she grabbed her chest with one hand. "What in the world are you doing here? It's Wednesday."

"It...it is my house, Naomi."

"No. You used to live here. It's not your night. Does Kendall know you're here?"

"You know we've been riding together." He bent and scooped up Kendall's laundry. "You're spoiling her by keeping everything together."

It was meant as a half-assed thank-you, but her expression turned deadly.

"I have the right to help my daughter and spoil her if I want. Someone needs to treat her nicely."

"I think I should head back outside." He tried to scoot around her, even with the laundry in his arms.

"I am dead set against you staying here. We have an arrangement and you're breaking it."

He dropped the laundry onto a dresser and turned back to the door. "I don't have an agreement with you, Naomi. There's not even a formal agreement between me and Kendall."

"I beg to differ."

"You can beg all you want, but as long as Kendall's comfortable with me at home, I'm staying. Now step aside, or I'll have to force you."

She did, cowering at the door as if he'd really threatened her.

Five years. For five years he'd been in the house,

been around her. He'd never hurt her, and he hoped she knew that.

"I'm truly sorry you don't want to be around me. After all this time, nothing's going to change that." He returned to his walk-in closet, jerked an old T-shirt out of a drawer. "I'm going to play with my daughter now. You can go talk with yours or complain. Whatever you want."

She moved to Kendall's dresser. With her back to him, she began refolding the laundry. He couldn't let her obvious hatred bring him down. Tonight was a plus. An extra night to see his daughter. More time with Kendall, with the possibility of a discussion.

Skylar Dawn was putting things away in her bedroom as her mother had instructed. He wouldn't interrupt her. Pulling his phone out, he texted his own mother. He hadn't appreciated her enough for accepting Kendall as part of their family. He had it pretty good.

His dad may not be capable of remembering things, but his mom was a rock. Just a simple Love you went a long way with her. The return text was a smiley face and heart emoji.

"Your ribs are cracked, aren't they?" Kendall appeared with an armful of kid stuff, probably from various places throughout the house.

"Did I forget to mention that? Yeah, it happened Sunday." He raised his shirt and let her see the darkening bruises. "It's getting better. How did you know?"

"You winced when Skylar Dawn jumped into your arms." She playfully acted like she was about to leap into his arms, too. "Bulls or broncs?"

"Bronc. He caught me off guard. I was thinking about something else."

"Dare I ask? I've seen all those rodeo groupies." She leaned against the doorframe and shook off an offer to help. "Never mind. It's none of my business."

"Wait a minute." He lowered his voice to avoid little ears. "I have never—okay, I can't say never. But since I've met you, I haven't been attracted to anyone else. What about you?"

"Oh, it's not like no one's asked," she teased. "It's just…there's something about touching the person you're in love with. That same kind of touch doesn't come from anyone else."

She smiled thoughtfully. Or maybe wistfully. Words weren't his thing. He'd always used as few as possible. But he'd never thought about what she'd said before. He liked it. She was exactly right. No forbidden fruit was better than a touch from her. No one affected him like she did.

His baby was done putting away her toys. He rushed in the room, squeaking like a monkey. Then he acted like the Wicked Witch of the West from *The Wizard of Oz*, quoting some of the famous lines from the movie. Skylar Dawn quickly imitated the monkeys and wanted to fly like them.

Kendall joined them by cackling and doot-da-do-da-doing the witch's theme. They all collapsed on the twin-size bed, tickling each other. Naomi walked by without a smile. No longer angry, he was simply sorry she couldn't find joy or happiness. He recognized the feeling.

When he wasn't with his family, he felt the same way.

THE EVENING WENT off without a hiccup—not one phone call about Marrone's questioning or Saundra Rosa's murder. No additional complications from Naomi, who left for her own home before dinner. And no last-minute inquiries from work, for either of them.

Heath glanced at his girls, his ladies, his loves. He slid the bookmark into *The Wizard of Oz* and snapped a picture of the page to be able to pick up the story if he read from his place.

Dammit. This was his place. Not the room he used at the Thompson's ranch.

Kendall didn't stir when he picked Skylar Dawn up from her arms. He tucked his daughter in bed, making sure the night-light wasn't blocked by a Lego tower. He kissed her forehead one more time before leaving her door cracked a couple of inches.

She'd be four years old next week.

And he'd missed six months of the past year.

To get to the guest room, he had to cross through the living room again. Kendall had slid down the leather couch and curled into a ball. He reached for a blanket but then tossed it into the chair he'd vacated.

Cracked ribs didn't deter him from lifting her into his arms and carrying her to their king-size bed. He left her dressed, but pulled a light blanket on top of her. He kissed her forehead and got a smile—he could see it from the night-light she now had in their room.

And because he couldn't resist the beautiful tempt-ress in front of him, he brushed her lips with his. He wouldn't be sleeping now. He could sit in her "perfect" chair that matched the "perfect" color of chocolate paint on the walls. Or he could lie down beside her.

Thunder rolled in the far distance as he watched the woman he loved sleep.

Chapter Fourteen

Kendall woke with something all too familiar wrapped around her...Heath. Lightning flashed. A crack of thunder followed.

At some point, Heath had moved them to the bedroom. She'd slept through it. Well, she might have missed him holding her earlier, but not now. His strong arm dropped from her shoulder to her waist.

Perfect. Her world right that minute was perfect.

"You okay?" he whispered close to her hair. His voice was so soft that it wouldn't have woken her. "Want me to go?"

"No. It's too late," she whispered. "You'd just come right back first thing. Stay. But I should check on Skylar Dawn."

"I got it." His warmth left her side as he rolled off the bed behind her.

Heath yawned, using a lot of his vocal chords, as he often did. It always made her smile. His bare feet slid across the carpet, then *tap-tap-tapped* down the hallway's wooden floor. Minutes slipped by. She closed her eyes, trying to reclaim the dream she'd been in. Heath returned, gently closing the door.

Another lightning bolt struck. The thunder answered more quickly. He sat in the chair they'd specially ordered to match the paint and bedspread.

"I don't mind sleeping on the couch." He crooked an arm behind his head, supporting it. He still had his white undershirt on along with the rest of his clothes. Another bolt of lightning gleamed off his championship-roping belt buckle.

Kendall pushed into a sitting position, letting the cover drop to her lap. "I need to get out of this blouse and bra."

"I could help with that if you're too tired." He was backlit by the glow of lights outside, so she relied on experience to know he grinned from ear to ear.

He wouldn't make the first move. He wouldn't say the first word, opening a conversation about what they really needed to discuss. When she'd suggested counseling six months ago, he'd told her talking had gotten them into this mess. Then he'd asked how it would get them out.

So far their week had been full of polite comments and—*dammit*—professionalism. Just like she'd insisted. God, she wanted to kiss him.

Wanted to lie next to his long body and be wrapped in his protectiveness. In five years, she'd never wanted to sleep alone. Before Heath, she'd never considered herself a cuddler. But she was. At least with him. And she missed it.

She threw back the covers and went to change. Their bathroom was in the opposite corner from where he sat. She didn't need the light to find the door or her things.

Her pj's hung on the hook. She slipped them on and crawled across the giant king-size bed back to her side.

If she'd walked over to her husband—still sitting in the chair—she would have sat on his lap, tucked her legs to her chest and wrapped her arms around his solid-as-a-rock chest.

But she hadn't. She pulled the covers up to her breasts, just wishing she had. Wishing for a simple way to get out of the mess they found themselves in.

"You'll be grumpy all day tomorrow if you sleep in that chair."

"I promise not to be grumpy." Heath's nails scratched the stubble on his cheek before running his fingers through his golden brown hair. It was a familiar movement that made her shiver in anticipation. She knew what his chin felt like against the softness of her skin.

"If you don't want to sleep on your side of the bed, just say so." Okay, that came out a bit snippy, but at least she'd gotten it out.

"You scared of the dark now?"

"Oh, the night-light? Your daughter has been coming to sleep with me. I think it's because you let her sleep with you."

Heath cleared his throat. The sound of fingers moving across his scalp seemed super loud in the silence.

"I'd probably be better off on the couch if you don't want me to touch you. I won't be able to make any promises to stay on my half of the bed." His voice was husky and, ironically, full of all sorts of promises.

"I don't recall asking you for any."

"Good. 'Cause I ain't giving any."

The click of the door locking got her hopes up even further. She felt his tall, lean body move through the room instead of heading for the couch.

Kendall covered her mouth, concealing her happy grin. She heard the boots hit the floor—first one, then the other. Another pause where he removed his socks. Heath stood in front of her, pulled his undershirt off, then dropped his old, torn jeans.

He'd lost weight if they fell off that easily. Lightning flashed, outlining his excellent physique. Anything he'd lost had turned to muscle.

"I'll never get back to sleep," she said as he dove over her to land in the middle of the bed.

"Do you need more sleep?"

"Don't you?"

The rain started then, and not a gentle spring sprinkle—it came pounding as hard as her heart. Light from the storm hung in the room long enough for her to see his jaw clench.

"I don't think sleep's in the cards tonight."

God, she hoped not.

They faced each other, both with an elbow propping them up, arms curled around a pillow. She waited for him to make the first move. Had he been serious? Or just teasing? He shifted on the bed, and yearning shot through her entire body at the memory of him lying there.

His free hand reached toward her to catch one of her pajamas' bowed strings. He playfully tugged. Untied, the front of his favorite silky pajamas would fall open like it had many times before. She hadn't thought what that might mean by way of an invitation when she'd hurriedly tugged them on. And now? Now she wanted the invitation to be loud and clear.

An excruciatingly slow pull finally had her top gaping open. The soft glow from outside the windows and the occasional burst of lightning showed her white breast right down to a hard nipple poking the green silk.

She wanted to roll Heath onto his back and take over. He'd let her. She could do what she wanted. But the exquisite turn-on of his exploration was as good as the very first time they'd made love.

She already ached and wanted out of her clothes. She wanted him. And under his boxers, she could tell he wanted her, too.

He gently rubbed the back of a knuckle across her nipple, sending a current through her body. One knuckle turned into four skimming back and forth, making her breath catch.

A half smile brightened Heath's face as the back of his hand slid across her belly, then a veiled touch moved across the inside of her arm, making her shiver. He laughed—a small sound that was full of the fun from torturing her.

She began to do the same to him, but he stopped her, pulling her fingers to his lips and kissing them one by one.

"That's not really fair."

"Nothing about this is fair," he mumbled against the inside of her wrist.

"Hmm? I'm relaxed now and think I can drift off again."

"Is that a challenge?" he asked, already moving to a sitting position and then to the end of the bed.

"Oh, I don't know." She deliberately yawned and lifted her arms above her head while turning on her back. "I'm seriously tired."

His hand wrapped around first one foot and then the other, dragging her entire body to line up with him at the end of the bed. "Toss it over here."

She slapped her hand backward on her headboard until she landed on the lotion bottle. Flipping it to him one-handed, she grinned to herself at how she'd obtained her foot massage.

Heath wasted no time kneading her tired feet, rubbing each part until she'd melted into the mattress.

"Would you relax?"

"I'm a marshmallow," she mumbled against the pillow.

"Only if the marshmallow's been in the sun and is all dried up." He tugged on her toes, wiggling them back and forth. But he was right. His strokes lengthened into long glides up her legs, with feather-soft kisses on the way back. His calloused fingers skimmed across her skin, exciting her entire body.

He stretched over her, capturing her hands above her head. Nuzzling the base of her neck, barely touching her with his lips, he then dragged the tip of his tongue to her shoulder. She wanted to squeal with delight at the way he caused her body to react.

She tugged at her hands and he let her go. She first pushed at his chest, then began to remove her pajama top. But his hands delayed her action, gently pushing her shoulders to the mattress.

All the while, the storm raged outside the thick-paned window. The lightning was more rapid now, followed by almost-constant rolling thunder. Rugged fingertips traced the outline of her pj top, dipping between her breasts to tease the delicate skin.

"You are absolutely beautiful." He fingered an errant strand of hair from her cheek. "I've missed you."

She parted her lips, about to quip that he'd been with her for four days, only to have Heath pull her quickly to him and slash his mouth across hers.

The temptation had been there each time they were close, but she'd held back. She'd missed kissing him. She didn't have to miss it anymore. They could figure out what would happen in the morning.

This very minute, she really needed him. All of him.

She stretched her arms around his back, wanting skin. Lots of skin. His body stretched on top of hers. He ran his hands down her sides, latching on to her hips and bringing them up to meet him.

He traced her collarbone with his mouth. "I love your legs. Love the fit of you against me." He emphasized his words by dropping his pelvis against hers.

Her mouth opened again and his tongue was there to pleasantly invade, dancing a dance that had stood the test of time. Without words, he invited her to join him.

Or maybe she'd been inviting him all along? She didn't care. She wanted her handsome man, and it was evident he wanted her. She slid her arms higher along his back. He quickly pushed himself up, taking the pressure of his chest from hers and lifting his back out of her reach. She immediately missed his warmth, his weight and…his everything.

His mouth seized her nipple through the silky material. He scraped his teeth gently over it, then captured her sensitive skin again. She bucked into him, wanting more. It didn't work. She could only accept the teasing and absorb the wonderful sensations building inside her.

Lying next to her again, he nudged her chin to turn with his knuckle. Once more he held her close, kissing her hard and excitedly, then soft and invitingly. Her breathing was fast and ragged. She forced her mouth away, letting the scruff on his chin rub her cheek. She hooked a finger on each side of his boxers and inched them lower on his hips.

Distant thunder. A gleam of far-off light. He quirked an eyebrow, questioning her, stopping his own exploration through her silky pajamas.

Keeping her eyes locked with his, she moved her hands to skim the light dusting of hair across his ruggedly hard chest. Again he stopped her. Was that her hand trembling or his?

"It's okay," she crooned, trying to convince them both. Convince them that everything would be fine for him, and that she knew what she was doing.

"I can still walk away, Kendall. I won't think a thing about this. Well, that's not true. I'll be disappointed, but I can still make it to the couch right now."

"I don't want you to go," she whispered. Then she kissed him, a long luxurious kiss that she had a hard time pulling away from.

"Will you let me stay?" he asked, his voice cracking with emotion.

Stay? As in…stay more than just tonight? As in, come home? Her mind shouted at her that they needed to talk, but her body drowned out the argument.

What really mattered was that she needed him.
Wanted him. Loved him.

"Stay."

Chapter Fifteen

Kendall looped a toe in the waistband of Heath's boxers and tugged them off his hips. He drew his breath, stupidly about to object, until she placed her fingertips across his lips.

"Shh."

Then came cool, confident kisses across his chin and shoulders and collarbone. His arms were getting weak supporting himself above her body. The look on her face told him she felt him tremble. The teasing Cheshire cat smile that followed issued a challenge.

It didn't take much to knock his arms aside and force him to drop on top of her. She surrounded him with her arms, using her nails to scrape his flesh in a sexy way only she could accomplish. Immediately, she soothed his skin with the soft brush of her fingertips.

God, her touch charged him with energy, rejuvenating his soul.

His hands grasped both sides of Kendall's hips to remove her pajama bottoms, then quickly shot to cup her face as he got caught up kissing his woman.

His. Everything about her was his. Missing her kept him up at night.

Their tongues tangled a brief moment before Kendall twisted and sat on top of him in the blink of an eye.

"Now, where was I before you distracted me with all that luscious kissing?"

Her hair was still in the tight ponytail like it had been every day recently. He hadn't seen it loose, felt it flow over him, in what seemed like forever. He reached and pulled off the holder.

He captured her surprised mouth and attacked her lips. When she moved, the long lengths of her legs caressed him like the silk of her pajamas.

He grasped her slender hips, his thumbs inching their way to her intimate secrets. She urged him to please her, and when she begged for release, he hesitated, savoring the magic of the way she looked.

Darkness seemed to penetrate everything in the room, but it was the first time in months Heath felt surrounded by light. It followed Kendall wherever she was—especially now. Her eyes were soft, her breasts lush, and the tip of her tongue peeked out between her lips. One last touch, and she cried out her release. The first of many, he hoped.

Lightning flashed, and he soaked in every long curvy line of her. Determined he would take his time, he savored every second of them together. But as the thunder rolled closer, shaking the windows with its intensity, Kendall guided him inside.

He was home…all he could do was feel. An overwhelming amount of love rushed through him, taking him to the only place he wanted to be.

"Don't move," he told her. "Just give me—"

She moved.

In a single motion, he flipped her to her back and let her pebbled nipples rub against his chest. Their hands were everywhere. Roaming, searching and exploring after being apart for six long months. He wanted to memorize every subtle change, wanted to feel her hair—

Kendall tried to move to one side, but he kept her where she was. With very little maneuvering, he slid into her again until the rhythm took care of itself. Kendall pulled him to her until they climaxed like the first days they were together.

Satisfied beyond words, Heath shifted to his side of the bed, bunching a pillow under his head. Kendall turned on her side, propping herself half on him and half on the mattress.

"Storm's moving on." He noticed the lightning flashes were fewer and farther apart.

"I suppose you're tired."

Was that another invitation? He softly dragged his fingers up and down her leg. He loved her soft skin. "Not really."

She nuzzled his wrist. He nuzzled her neck in return. He laughed, and the sound was short but deep from his core. It was an excellent new start, even without an official apology from either of them. But there was plenty of time for that. Now that he would be around every day again.

"What did you have in mind?" he asked after she twined her legs around his.

"We could make up for lost time."

"Actually, I need some food before we go a second

round." He twisted a little to get a look at her. "We didn't have dinner. Aren't you starving?"

"Oh." She pursed her lips together in a short pout and kissed him. "Mister, you talk entirely too much. Do you know that?" She turned over, scooting her body into a spooning position.

He'd missed his opportunity to make up for lost time. She was ready for sleep. His right arm was tugged over her body as she pulled her hair out of the way to rest on his left biceps. "Okay, yeah, I get it. You want to cuddle. I can handle that."

A deep type of hunger had been satiated by Kendall. He could wait until morning breakfast with Skylar Dawn to satisfy the other. No food was worth moving away from his wife. He enjoyed her this close.

Life was complete.

IT WAS MUCH earlier than anyone normally got up, but Heath didn't mind. He woke up and decided to run home for a different suit. But that didn't work. As soon as he was out of their bedroom, he heard Skylar Dawn reading under the covers.

Whether she was actually reading was still a mystery. She at least had the book she'd memorized last year with a flashlight pointed at it. She was reading all the parts with different voices for the mommy, daddy and little girl.

Since neither of them could head back to bed, he decided to make breakfast. He still had clean shirts hanging in his closet. Who needed a different suit when he had an opportunity to spend time with his daughter?

"Does MiMi have to pick me up?" Skylar Dawn asked between bites of scrambled eggs.

"Yes. Mommy and I still have to go to work." He flipped a Spanish omelet for Kendall.

"But I like it when you pick me up."

"Why? Want to get dirty?" He gently tapped her nose with his knuckle.

"No, silly." She pointed her fork at him. "We go see Stardust. I love my pony. Can we go today?"

"Sure thing. But we have to go to work first."

"I don't work." She giggled.

"You do your work at day care."

The oven timer began to ring in an old-fashioned buzz. He'd have to replace that ancient thing before long.

"Biscuits ready!" Skylar Dawn shouted.

Heath stuck the spatula over his lips. "Hey, Mom had a late night."

"Biscuits," his daughter whispered, pointing to the oven door. "I want cotton jelly."

"Cotton jelly it is." He laughed. Cotton was short for apricot. They'd all called it that since Skylar Dawn had first asked for it that way.

He spread the jelly on thick, and Skylar Dawn had it on both sides of her cute little mouth when Kendall came into the kitchen.

"What's this? Everybody's up so early." She kissed their daughter's forehead, swiping a finger of jelly off a sticky cheek before turning to him. "You made breakfast."

"Daddy made it special." Skylar Dawn pointed to the stove.

Heath rushed to the pan, pushing it off the burner before the omelet burned. "It's not much."

"I think it's super." She wet some paper towels and cleaned up their baby girl.

Why did he get the feeling something was wrong?

"Everything okay?" he asked, almost afraid of the answer.

"Go make your bed and brush your teeth. Then you can watch TV until it's time to go." She helped Skylar Dawn off the barstool and watched her leave the room.

Heath set down two plates with half of a badly formed omelet on each, then two cups of the single-serving coffee. Then he sat down himself. Kendall leaned against the wall leading to the open living room.

"Going to eat?"

"I'm not really hungry."

"We've got a full day today and might not have time for lunch. You might—"

"I can decide when I want to eat, Heath."

No need for guessing. She was upset. Maybe even angry.

He accidentally dropped his fork on the floor. He bent to get it, but Kendall beat him. She walked it to the sink and didn't turn around to face him.

"Maybe you should take your own advice and just tell me what you want, instead of writing a book in your head to find the best words."

"Okay." She spun around. "I've been offered a promotion. It's an opportunity to lead a cybercrime group."

"And it's in Portland." He should have known.

"How did you know? Oh, the phone call."

"Are you taking it?" His knees hadn't buckled. That was good.

"I... I don't know."

"Are you telling me about it or asking?"

"What do you mean?"

He pushed away from the bar, scooped up the plates and headed for the garbage. He no longer had an appetite either.

"Telling me means you're moving and asking me for a divorce." He rinsed and placed the plates in the dishwasher. "Asking me means you'd like me to come along."

"I haven't... I don't know yet."

"Are you asking or telling?" he pressed again.

He couldn't look at her or he'd lose it. Really lose it. As in yell that she couldn't go. He watched her reflection in the window as she covered her face with one hand and wrapped the other tight around her waist.

Exactly where his arm had been all night.

"If last night hadn't happened, how long would you have waited to tell me you were leaving?"

"That's not fair." She swallowed hard and faced the counter—away from him. "I need to think."

Fair? Think? What about his life had been fair in the past six months? He'd said what he felt at the time, before thinking it through. Before realizing that it hadn't been what he meant.

He wanted Kendall to quit work when *she* wanted to quit. He wanted her only to be happy. As many times as he'd told her that before he'd left, she obviously hadn't really believed him.

Heath didn't have words. How could they work with

this hanging over their heads all day? He didn't know what to do.

The hell he didn't. He was taking the day off.

"You know, Kendall. I think this is the perfect day for Skylar Dawn to play hooky. Tell your mom she's got the weekend off."

"You can't—"

"Darlin', I can." He left the kitchen, calling to his daughter. "Skylar Dawn, change of plans. Get your boots, darlin'. Let's go see Stardust and Jupitar."

He got his daughter out of the house quickly by throwing a few things into her backpack and setting her on his hip.

When she asked, he told their girl that her mommy wasn't feeling well. It wasn't a lie. He was pretty sure that Kendall felt real bad about springing it on him like that.

Last night had been a natural reaction. Something neither of them had expected, but they'd both wanted it. Maybe she'd been conflicted. Maybe they shouldn't have made love.

He didn't have the answers, and apparently neither did Kendall.

Chapter Sixteen

"Are we really staying here all weekend, Daddy?" Skylar Dawn kicked the ribs of her pony to keep up with his mare.

"Yepper doodles," he said in a bad cartoon duck voice.

She laughed. "And I get to ride Stardust every day? And not go to school? And I get to stay at the ranch house? And we get to order pizza?"

"Yeppers on everything, but I think Mama Thompson is making the dough. Then you can make your own pizza in her oven."

"I can put as much cheese on it as I want?"

"I'll leave that to Mama Thompson to decide."

"This is fun, Daddy."

"Yepper doodles."

She laughed at him again.

They'd gotten to the Thompson ranch early. He'd taken care of feeding the other horses and had let Skylar Dawn feed the chickens. The Thompsons had come to the paddock to say hello and get their order for lunch.

Both adults had seen through his excuse that Kendall wasn't feeling well. They told him several times they'd be hanging around the ranch all weekend if he needed help. They'd had a short, knowing look with each other, then Slate's mom had told him she'd make all his favorites.

"Is Mama Thompson my grandmother?"

"Not really, darlin'. But she loves you like a grand-daughter."

"I like it here."

By "here" she meant the Thompson ranch, large fields surrounded by trees that cut them off from the housing developments. A secret little stock pond full of catfish. Far enough away from the major roads a person couldn't tell they were twenty minutes from the Dallas suburbs.

He slowed Jupitar to a stop, letting Stardust have a little break. Tipping his hat, he shoved his hair back from his face. Maybe they should go for haircuts this afternoon. Or fishing. Skylar Dawn usually screamed and giggled at live bait, but she was surprisingly patient for an almost-four-year-old.

Shoot, she'd be four in nine days.

Skylar Dawn imitated him by taking off her little straw cowgirl hat, shoving her bangs back and securing it again on her cute little head. He'd been corrected more than once that she was a girl, not a boy.

"Fishing or the barber shop? Which do you want to do after pizza?"

He'd let Skylar Dawn decide. This was her day to play hooky and his to wonder about their future.

"Pizza, then Mr. Craig at the candy shop."

The old-fashioned barber pole looked like a candy cane. He didn't bother to correct her. It didn't matter.

How many days would they have like this if Kendall moved them to Portland?

His wife would transfer, get the promotion she'd longed for. He'd have to seek out a new job in law enforcement. Go through more training, be reduced to rookie status—man, he didn't look forward to that.

Dad-blast it. He'd have to give up the horses. Moving them would be too hard. Paying for them even harder. His daughter was just getting the hang of riding, too. They were almost at the edge of the property.

Where had the time gone? Out of the corner of his eye, he caught Skylar Dawn rocking in the saddle. This was probably the longest she'd been in it. No matter, he'd let her ride with him on the way back. That would help.

"My, my, my," she said, sitting back in her saddle like him. "Have you and Mother had another fight?"

"What? Since when do you call Mommy 'Mother'?" He knew the answer. His mother-in-law always said "my, my, my," so this had to be her insistence on proper English. Never mind that. He needed to answer the real question. "Why do you think we had a fight?"

"You're acting funny, Daddy."

He guided Jupiter to face both Skylar Dawn and her little pony. What could he say to make her feel better? No lies. He refused to do it. But he also refused to make his daughter's life miserable.

"Hey, baby. Sometimes things go wrong. So, yeah, Mommy and I argued. But that doesn't mean we don't love you or each other. Remember that time you had a fight with Stacy? What was that about?"

"Bumble. She said he had a stupid name. We aren't supposed to say *stupid* in school."

"That's right. But you still went to play at her house that Saturday."

She nodded her sweet little head. "You and Mommy are still friends, too?"

"Always. No matter what."

"Okay." She shrugged, pulling the reins to go around him.

Dammit. No matter what happened…

Friends, lovers, parents. They'd always be all of those things. There was nothing else to think about. He'd follow Kendall to Portland. He'd live with her or live next door—whatever she wanted. Not just for Skylar Dawn. He'd be there for his wife until she told him differently.

"Daddy?"

Heath wiped the bit of raw emotion from his eyes. Putting a smile on his face, he looked Skylar Dawn in the eyes. "What, honey?"

"What's that?" She pointed behind him.

He turned in his saddle and saw a dust cloud.

Dust? After all the rain they'd had last night? Not dust. *Exhaust!*

"I don't know, sweetheart."

Woah. Engines. The sound of all-terrain vehicles echoed off the stock pond's built-up back containment wall. There were several of them. The Thompsons had only one.

This was not good. Something was off.

"Hey, baby girl, I think you need to ride with Daddy for a while." He guided Jupitar next to Stardust, then reached down to lift Skylar Dawn. Setting her in front of him, he looped his left arm around her.

"You're squeezing too tight, Daddy."

"We're going to go fast, baby. You like fast, right?"

"Yes!"

Excited, she grabbed Jupitar's mane, ready to fly. Now if he just had someplace to go. At the edge of the property, there weren't any back gates close by. Even if he had wire cutters in his back pocket, he couldn't cut the barbed wire before those four-wheelers caught up with him.

He kicked Jupitar into motion. The mud might slow down the men headed their way, but not his mare. She was as fast as the lightning that had cut across the sky in the early morning hours.

"Hang on, baby!"

He'd loped horses with his girl sitting there a couple of times, but not as fast as this. He tugged her to him even closer. There wasn't any doubt the vehicles were following them. Thank God he knew what he was doing.

Riding this land every day had him knowing just where to go. He could make it harder for them to follow. Lead them into small ditches that might be bogged down with mud.

"Stop before you hurt your daughter!"

What the hell?

A gunshot pierced the sound of the galloping hooves. He couldn't slow down enough to tell if they were really aiming at them or not. Mud shot up from Jupitar's legs. The wind whipped their faces as the sun beat down, warming them. His mare darted to the right, causing him to rise in his saddle.

Skylar Dawn screamed. "Daddy, slow down!"

"I can't, baby. I can't."

Public Exposure! The information they'd obtained must have scared them into going after all of Kendall's family. It was the only explanation. He hadn't been on any major Ranger cases. No one was after him. It had to be Brantley Lourdes.

"Haw!" he shouted to Jupitar.

No use trying to get his cell out of his back pocket. Both hands were occupied controlling Jupitar and holding on to Skylar Dawn.

If he could just make it back to the house…

That's when he saw another vehicle. He hadn't turned around to see how many four-wheelers had followed. They'd split up, boxing him in.

He could try to jump the fence, but Jupitar wasn't a jumper. More likely, she'd dump them over her head by coming to a full stop. The vehicle got closer. Two hooded men rode it. One carried a shotgun.

No choices.

No options.

"Whoa, girl." He pulled Jupitar to a stop.

"Daddy?"

He might have halted, but he didn't ease his grip on his daughter.

"First things first. Toss your cell on the ground. Careful-like. Make sure it's face up, and no monkey business." The voice was full of authority and came from behind him.

He slid his hand down the reins, lengthening his grip until he could reach behind him. He tossed it, forcing the man to get off the back of the ATV in front of Heath and pick it up. The man cracked the case, removed the SIM card and then threw it over the fence.

Jupitar startled. He whistled to get her under control. The man with the shotgun jumped off the ATV and pointed it at the horse. *No! Them.*

Skylar Dawn was between the barrel and his chest. There were too many, and he was unarmed. "Down on your own or we can pull you off of there, Ranger," the guy behind Heath said.

There was always the slim chance that the Thompsons had seen the ATVs come up the drive. A slim chance…but a chance nonetheless.

"I don't know who you are, but point the gun away from my daughter."

"There's one way this is going to go. Mine. If you do as I say, we'll be glad to point our weapons at only you. Now, get down," the guy behind him directed.

"I'm scared, Daddy." Skylar Dawn had a death grip on his arm. "Why can't we see their faces?"

"It'll be okay, sweetheart."

"Only if you do as I say," the guy doing all the talking said.

"I can get him down," said the one still straddling the ATV in front of Heath.

"Come on, Heath, get off your high horse." A second man behind him chuckled. "Listen to me, or I'll have to kill you in front of your kid."

"Trauma does weird things to kids, man," a third voice said from behind him. "Just look at all of us."

They all laughed and agreed. Skylar Dawn began to cry. He couldn't turn around to see who was there. But looking toward the house, he could tell no one would come there in time to stop these men from doing what they wanted.

No choices.

No options.

Unsure exactly how much his daughter understood, Heath switched her around to face him. "Hold on to Daddy, hon." Her little hands latched behind his neck, and he kicked his leg around until it looped around the saddle horn. It was a tricky place to balance, especially with a small child.

"Steady, girl," he instructed Jupitar.

His left arm held his shaking daughter—who was holding it together much better than he'd ever thought possible. The other held the edge of his saddle. He needed something. Some type of defense. His fingers searched for his rope.

"Whoa there, partner," one of them said. "Keep your hands where we can see them."

"I have to get down, right?"

"Want me to get the girl, boss?"

"That's not necessary. Heath Murray is a champion cowboy. I bet he can slide to the ground from where he's at."

Heath's boots hit the ground, and his horse didn't move. He was out of stall tactics, out of ideas. What did they want? Was it a ploy to scare him or did they—

Stardust came into view, being led by yet another man in a mask. That made six he could now see. Three ATVs with two men each. None of them had identifying marks. No unusual clothing. He couldn't even tell skin color. They either had on goggles, or the skin around their eyes was blacked out like superheroes on TV.

"That's right, Heath. You're surrounded and have no

options. Get her." The main guy pointed to one of the men and then to Heath's daughter.

Heath wanted to back up, to run. But the leader was right. He was surrounded.

"Hold on now!" he shouted and put Skylar Dawn's back toward Jupitar's neck. "Why are you doing this? What do you want?"

"Hell, Heath. I thought we were pretty clear about that. We want your daughter. We made a special trip out here and everything," he joked.

"Whatever reason you have for doing this, just tell me. We can come up with some kind of a deal."

"A Texas Ranger like you? Married to an FBI agent? I don't think so." He pointed again—this time at the man holding the shotgun. "Shoot the pony." The man swung the gun from Heath to Stardust.

He tried covering his daughter's eyes, but her little fingers tugged at his hand. She screamed. She twisted.

"No! Stop! Daddy, don't let them hurt Stardust!"

The man pumped a shell into the chamber. It didn't matter. He'd never drop his daughter. How could he?

Three men got to Heath. Two tugged his arms. The third tore his now-hysterical daughter from him. She screamed, "Daddy! Stardust! Don't you hurt them! Stop! Daddy! Help!"

One man locked Heath's arms behind his back. Another hit him. He threw them off. Tried to get to Skylar Dawn. She kicked and twisted herself and bit the man's wrist until she wiggled to the ground and ran. Heath ran after her but was tripped.

He fell, eating mud, as he yelled for his daughter. She was scooped up, her little legs still running through the air. Her hands in little fists beat on the leg of her attacker.

One of the men kicked him in the back of his head. Then again in his sore ribs. White-hot light radiated through every part of him as he heard the rib crack on the second kick. He tried to get his feet under him, but again the toe of a shoe hit him in the side. He began coughing, unable to catch his breath.

The ATV engines revved to life. He couldn't hear his daughter. Maybe because they had gagged her, or maybe because a buzzing sound was shooting between his ears.

One by one the engine sounds faded. He coughed, choked. He couldn't see because of the mud covering his face. Could feel only the pain from his heart breaking.

"Skylar Dawn," he called.

He wasn't alone. Something moved through the brush close to him. One of the men was still there—their leader. He grabbed Heath's shirt, dragging him to his feet and hitting him. How many times, he didn't know.

The world was just pain. It was worse than being trampled by a bull. Much worse. The leader shoved him to the ground. Heath couldn't move.

"We'll be in touch," the bastard said over him. "Follow our directions or you'll never see her again."

The third engine roared loudly to life and then faded across the field. Heath used his shoulder to get a bit of the mud from his eyes. He rolled, taking a long while to get to his knees.

"Oh God." He fought through the pain. Fought to stay awake.

If he could just get to Jupitar. And then what? He tripped over something on the ground and fell hard, taking the brunt of the fall with his chest. He couldn't scream. Couldn't call out. Could barely breathe.

His eyes focused on a small straw hat near his face. "I'll find you, baby girl. And those bastards will pay."

Chapter Seventeen

"Where is he? Come on, Heath. Pick up." Kendall looked at her phone as if it had the answer. Then she dialed Slate's number and quickly hung up when Jerry walked up.

"Glad you could get here so fast, Kendall." Jerry did a finger gesture pointing to her cell. "Is there something wrong? Having trouble with Heath?"

"No. Did you find something on the thumb drive?"

"Look, I was your partner a long time. It sounded like you were looking for your husband. Is he MIA or do you know where he is?"

"I'm sure everything's fine and he's not answering because he's knee-deep in muck at the ranch."

"Okay. There's nothing yet on the encryption. I came over to see how you were and tell you that you're needed in the conference room."

Jerry left but the creepy feeling didn't as she walked to her summons. Something was wrong. People could call it whatever they wanted, but she just knew something was off.

"Thanks for coming in, Special Agent Barlow." Steve

Woods opened the door to the conference room and gestured for her to sit. "Is Ranger Murray not with you?"

"No, sir. He had…obligations today." She hoped those obligations would allow him to call her soon.

"I wanted to introduce you to Agent Therese Ortis. She'll be taking over the Marrone interrogation. It seems your local complaints have backed into her ongoing investigation."

"Of Public Exposure?"

"Yes," Agent Ortis said. She stood at the other end of the room, arms crossed, mainly looking into a two-way mirror. "I can't go into many details. Sorry about that. I know how frustrating it can be."

Kendall had known from the beginning that the company she'd been investigating had ulterior motives. She just hadn't been able to connect anything except the local dots.

"We wanted you to know that Marrone was released late last night. His lawyer argued it was an illegal stop." The second-in-command of the Dallas field office took a step to the door.

"What about the parole violation? Didn't we have him on that?" She looked from one agent to the other. "This would be one of those things I can't know?"

"You did a good job," Agent Ortis acknowledged.

"Then why do I feel like I'm being punished?" She shook their hands. "Am I off the case?" she asked.

"Therese might have additional—"

"Actually, I'd like to work with Special Agent Barlow—that is, with your permission—wherever I can." She crossed the room with her hand extended. "There are some things I won't be able to fill you in on. At least not yet."

"Thank you. I'd be glad to help." Her phone buzzed in her jacket pocket. "Is that all, sir?"

He nodded, and she left the room to answer. She returned to her desk and redialed Slate Thompson.

"Kendall?"

Finally. "I've been leaving messages everywhere. I need to talk—"

"Hey, yeah, about that. I got your messages and called the ranch. Mom took a look and found Stardust, Skylar Dawn's pony. She returned to the paddock. Alone. Then Jupiter ran up. I'm on my way there now. I'll call you as soon as I know anything."

It all happened in slow motion.

Kendall looked up to see agents running toward her. She hadn't realized she'd dropped to her knees, taking a stack of files to the floor with her.

Skylar Dawn was gone or hurt? Where was Heath? She'd known something was wrong. She couldn't speak. Her throat seemed to be connected to every part of her body and it was all shutting down, vital organ by vital organ. Someone helped her to stand, and she felt a chair at the back of her knees.

Voices talked over one another. Someone called for assistance. The room filled with men and women. All the dark suits seemed to fade to black.

Kendall took it all in, struggling to think. She stared at her colleagues. None of them could really help. She couldn't keep her daughter safe. Heath might be hurt.

"What happened?" Jerry asked. "Someone call a paramedic."

"Something's wrong. What if they took Skylar Dawn? Heath's… I don't know what's happened and I have a terrible feeling."

"Someone find out what she's talking about. And where the hell are the paramedics?"

"I'm not hurt. I have to get to the ranch." She shoved herself to her feet, rolling the chair backward, hitting someone who stood behind her.

"Kendall, you aren't making sense," someone said. She didn't know who, and didn't have time to figure it out.

She moved through a throng of agents, all clueless how to help. She did an about-face. "I need my Glock." She ran back to her desk and slid her weapon into its holster.

"You aren't going anywhere alone. I'll drive you. That's not a question. You aren't leaving without me." Jerry took her elbow and guided her from the building.

Again, time passed at a snail's pace. Couldn't Jerry drive faster?

Where was the fast-forward button? It had been only a blink of an eye since her daughter was born. One little skip, and now they were planning her fourth birthday party. She needed time to move at the same rate now.

Her phone vibrated in her pocket. "Heath?"

"It's me," Slate said. "Heath's unconscious. We've called for an ambulance."

"And Skylar Dawn?"

"She's not here."

"Are you arranging a search party?"

"Kendall, Heath was attacked. He's really bad off. We found tire tracks."

"Are you saying my daughter was kidnapped?"

There was a long pause. Jerry flipped the lights to warn cars to get out of the way.

"I'm on my way."

SITTING ON THE PORCH, Heath listened as Slate tried to issue orders indoors. Jerry Fisher and Major Clements were arguing. Both wanted their respective agencies to be in charge of the investigation. Law enforcement officers searched the area, but they wouldn't find anything. He'd told them that.

Skylar Dawn had been kidnapped by Public Exposure. No doubt in his mind about that. Two hours had passed, and still no word. Drained, his body ran on autopilot, sipping a cup of coffee Mama Thompson had put in his hands.

The idea that someone would hurt his daughter kept replaying in his mind, caught on an endless repeating loop. He couldn't stop it.

"Yes, Ranger Murray is conscious, but the kidnappers wore masks. He said there were six men." Slate was speaking to someone in the living room.

Heath had lost track. Everyone was involved. Local PD, Rangers, Public Safety, FBI Dallas and surrounding departments—they were holding off on issuing an Amber Alert. And he sat there…doing nothing except holding a cup of coffee. He couldn't bring himself to even drink.

"The paramedics said you should go to the hospital, son." Slate's dad laid a kind, gentle hand on his shoulder.

"I'm good."

"You need X-rays. What if you've punctured a lung or something? What good will you be to your little girl then?"

Heath took a deep breath, letting it out slowly. His eyes met Kendall's. "Nope. I'm good."

He hadn't really spoken to Kendall. He hadn't told

her he was sorry for not protecting Skylar Dawn. He took a sip. The breeze across the porch was cool today.

"Did someone find her hat?" he asked. The words came out, but he thought they sounded weird. Maybe it was a weird thing to worry about. "She's going to want her hat."

Kendall moved to sit next to him. "Her hat is with the little bit of evidence they found."

"I told all of them they didn't leave anything."

"They took seven sets of footprints, the ATV tire tracks. But nothing that will point us in the right direction."

"No one knew I was here, Kendall. I should have been working with you. Slate and his parents saw me this morning. That's it. I asked them not to mention us if you called. Sorry about that."

She shook her head.

"Why do you think it was Public Exposure?" Kendall's voice dropped to just above a whisper.

"It's logical after this week. They were organized. They listened to one guy. We know something's happening in their organization. You have the flash drive. They obviously don't want you to discover what's on it. Then they kidnap our daughter."

A cell phone rang. From across the porch, they heard Slate answer. "Ranger Thompson."

Slate ran over to them. "It's the kidnapper. He'll only talk to Heath. No speaker."

The bastard had his daughter. He wanted to curse, rant, say a hundred things, but he kept his mouth shut. Slate placed the phone in his hand.

"Ranger Murray?"

"I'm here. What do you want?"

"Your daughter or your wife. You choose."

During the long pause that followed, Heath wondered if the man had hung up. "You must choose, Ranger. Your daughter? Or your wife? Which will it be? I'll telephone again."

"Wait! Is Skylar—" The call disconnected. "Dammit!"

"What? What did he... Is she okay? Did she say anything?" Kendall stayed next to him.

Others gathered close. He wanted to tell Kendall that everything would be all right, but he didn't know if it was true. He desperately clung to whatever courage he had left. Courage that kept him from collapsing like a desperate father, while Kendall held it all together. Another mother would have fallen apart long before now.

"He wants me to choose between you and Skylar Dawn."

"There's no choice." Her gaze held his.

"You're damn right! I can't choose. I won't."

Kendall cupped his face. "I'm not asking you to. I already have. We're doing everything exactly as he says. We have to if we want to see Skylar Dawn again. She needs to be safe."

Half of him knew she meant it. The other half of him couldn't believe her logical, matter-of-fact response. None of him believed she would've asked such a thing of him.

"Right. How do we convince them?" He nodded toward the men scattered all over the Thompsons' lawn.

"Tell me again what he said. Word for word."

HEATH SAT ON the porch and repeated the short phone call word for word. Then he sat in the living room and repeated it. Then he repeated the conversation in the dining room. He answered all the questions they asked with an "I don't know." He couldn't take it anymore. He grabbed Kendall's hand, leaning on her a bit more than his masculinity preferred.

They left the porch and the crowds. Kendall released his hand and draped his arm around her neck.

"Thanks. Not keeping my feet under me is kind of embarrassing."

People kept reminding him there'd been six men and a gun pointed at his daughter. Hearing it over and over didn't help.

"Where are we heading?" she asked.

"The barn. I don't think anyone's unsaddled Jupitar and Stardust."

"Okay." She didn't try to change his mind, but she did wrap her arm around his hip and take more of his weight.

They walked together and he gained more strength. It was better than sitting around, listening to the different law enforcement agencies argue about who was in charge. Bottom line—he and Kendall would decide how to move forward. Skylar Dawn was their little girl.

"It's going to be hard to fight the bad guys in my current physical condition."

She released him to lean on the corral rail, then pointed to his horses at the water trough. "I don't think you can unsaddle, feed and rub down both horses. But I bet Mr. Thompson would care for them."

"I'll ask him." He reached for his cell. "Dammit, they

destroyed my phone. It's somewhere in the neighbor's field, or collected for evidence."

"Sorry, the FBI took mine to trace any possible incoming calls."

"You know that I'm… It was my fault. I'm the one who's sorry." He cupped her face with his hands, staring into the sadness in her eyes. "If only I hadn't brought her here. There just wasn't anything I could do when they showed up."

She wrapped her hands around his wrists, holding him where he was. "I know. We all know. My God, Heath, there were six of them. You're lucky to be alive."

"If anything happens to her…"

"You heard what the kidnappers said. They wouldn't have said anything about me unless I'm the one they really want." She cupped his cheeks like he still held hers. "Promise me you'll go after Skylar Dawn. You do whatever they tell you to do and find her."

She looked at him expectantly. He nodded. The promise just wouldn't come. He'd find a way. He had to.

"Do you hear that?" he asked.

"It sounds like a cell phone. Wait here."

Kendall ran into the barn. Then grabbed Stardust, leading her inside. He waited. The barn had been cleared by three agencies. Nothing would harm her there. It was easier than attempting to catch up. Physically, he felt better than he had two hours ago, but he needed time to recover—something they didn't have much of.

"Heath!" she called.

He limped his way through the door and heard the cell phone. It was tucked under the edge of Skylar Dawn's saddle.

"There are clear bags in the tack room." He pointed.

"Do you think it's them?" She ran, shouting over her shoulder.

"It has to be. None of the men clearing the scene would have left their cell."

Once back, she carefully slid the phone from the pony as he lifted the saddle.

"We have a choice here, Heath. We answer it and move forward, possibly on our own. Or we let the FBI set up the trace and answer it the next time it rings. And to be honest…I don't know which is the best way to go."

"Does it say there are any missed calls?"

"Not that I can see, but that doesn't mean anything, Heath. It might not be programmed to show that. How could all those agents have missed this?"

The phone stopped ringing. He shrugged while looking into the corners of the barn. He couldn't see anything. There were too many places to look for hidden cameras. But he knew.

"They're watching us, Kendall. I can feel it. They were here." He pointed to his feet. "Probably here in the barn. They waited for one of us to come here to the barn to call."

"You can't be sure—"

The phone rang again. He stretched for the plastic-covered cell.

She met his hand with her own, reaching across Stardust. "That was the FBI agent talking. Kendall Barlow trusts you." She scooted the ringing phone out of the plastic enough to push the green answer button and then speaker.

"It's about time," the same voice from earlier said.

"I've got a couple of errands for you. There won't be another call, so you better remember. You with me?"

"Yes," they both answered.

"There are no exceptions. Keep this phone. I'll call you tonight to give you further instructions. You'll need a black suit and a bright red dress. No exceptions. There's a wedding reception at the Anatole Hotel tonight. Be there."

The phone went dead, and they stared at each other.

"They'll never let us do this on our own."

"This guy didn't even ask us not to involve the cops." As inconspicuously as possible, he looked around the barn again.

"It would be impossible to assume we wouldn't find a way."

"Kendall, he didn't ask for anything."

"Except me."

The grip they both had on each other's hand was rock solid. They hadn't been unified in a long time, but there wasn't any question they were now. They'd follow the kidnapper's instructions. They'd get their little girl back.

And somehow, he'd save Kendall, too.

Chapter Eighteen

Fancy red dress? Check. Black suit, white dress shirt? Check. Boots for the suit? On Heath's feet. Small clutch purse with the Cherry Bomb lipstick she'd bought ages ago to match the dress? Check.

Jeans and T-shirts for them both...just in case. And a change of clothes for her daughter. Red high heels?

"Mother, where are my red high heels?" In a flash, she remembered that Heath had given those to Company B to attach a tracker. "Never mind."

Everything was beside their bag. Just like it was supposed to be. She went over the list a second time, unable to accept that it was complete. It was a simple list and a simple task. Her mother had pulled everything together and laid it out on the end of Kendall's bed.

Their bed—hers and Heath's.

In spite of checking the list twice—make that three times—she had the nagging feeling that she had forgotten something.

"You're forgetting your jewelry," her mother said, coming up behind her and sniffing into her tissue. "You really shouldn't go to a wedding without any jewelry. It will look odd."

"That's it." She removed her wedding rings and walked to her vanity to put them away.

"I meant that you can't attend an evening wedding without jewelry, darling. Not to take your rings off."

"I don't want to lose them."

She dropped her ring set on the porcelain hand Skylar Dawn had given to her. Or, more accurately, Heath had given it to her for her first Mother's Day gift.

"Would they do that? They'd not only kidnap your daughter, they'd steal your wedding rings?"

"I don't know what they'll do, Mother. This is a first for me, too."

Her mother gathered the extra clothes she'd set out, placing them in a garment bag. Kendall couldn't remember owning one. Taking a step toward the door she stopped herself. She'd been heading to Skylar Dawn's room again.

It was silly how long she'd just sat there, staring at the half-built Lego castle. She wanted to finish it for her daughter. But they were working on it together. She couldn't touch a piece without Skylar Dawn telling her where it went. That was the rule.

Kendall returned to her vanity instead and reapplied her eye makeup. It was getting close to the time Heath's partner would pick them up. She should go check on him. But twenty minutes ago, he'd drifted fitfully off to sleep. Obviously still in pain, but refusing to take anything that would impair his judgment.

Her mother watched from the doorway of the bathroom. She was sighing a lot, a cue that she wanted to say something.

"Thanks for staying here, Mother. There will be agents outside. You'll be perfectly safe."

"I'm not worried about that." She lifted a finger, indicating that Kendall should join her in the bedroom.

A sinking feeling hit between her shoulders. She wouldn't like what her mother was about to say. "Are you sure this can't wait, Mother?"

"You've got plenty of time, I think. Heath isn't awake yet."

"It might be better—"

"I need you to promise me something, dear."

"I promise I won't do anything stupid." Used to this promise, Kendall said it without thinking much about it. Her mother required it every week or so. Did it matter that this time she didn't believe that anything would truly keep her out of harm's way tonight?

"No, dear. I need you to promise that when you bring my granddaughter back to me, you'll finally restrict that man's visitation to supervisory visits only."

She could only stare at her mother.

What?

Helpless. Stunned. She couldn't think of words. Her daughter had been taken in order to draw her out without a fight. She might not ever see her baby again. Might not see anyone again for that matter. The demand from her mother struck her as ridiculous.

"I don't understand, Mother."

Naomi Barlow perched on the edge of the chair, prime and proper with her hands on her knees. "You can't trust that man. This would never have happened if Skylar Dawn had been here, where she belonged."

"They would have taken her from day care or even

here. There's no telling how many additional people would have been hurt if that had happened. This is not Heath's fault. How can you blame him?"

"He comes and goes as he pleases."

"It's his house."

"I know he spent last night in this room and not the guest room."

"This is not the time, Mother."

"He took our girl without even telling you where he was going, disrupting her routine."

"Getting her dirty?" The deep voice came from the doorway.

Kendall sent a look telling him to cool it. But she didn't blame him. A lot had happened. Just a few days earlier, her mother hadn't allowed him to say good-night to his daughter. And before they could bring their baby home Naomi wanted her to commit to what? A divorce?

Heath did a one-eighty and left. She wanted to follow, but enough was enough.

"Heath is my husband, Mother. He's the father of my child. If anything happens to me tonight, he has the right to limit your involvement in Skylar Dawn's life. And frankly, I wouldn't blame him. I can't believe you could even think about cutting him out of our lives. How could you?" She headed for the door, but her mother's sobbing stopped her.

"Oh my goodness. I… This can't be happening. It just can't be happening." Her mother cried for real now.

"But it is, Mom. It's not Heath's fault. There were six men attacking him. He could have been killed." She lowered her voice, almost choking to get the words out.

"I… I thought he was dead. I would never have forgiven myself."

She turned quickly to hide the tears. Her gaze fixed on her engagement ring. She'd never planned to marry. Everything about her life had been about joining the FBI. As a little kid, she'd always thought she'd find her father. She'd quickly outgrown that idea as she went through high school and college, each course chosen as a precursor to joining the academy. Every extracurricular activity was carefully chosen for the same reason.

She'd run cross-country for stamina. Even been on the college wrestling team. She'd been in such control of her future, securing the job with the FBI. Then she'd met Heath, and everything had changed.

No more rigid control. Instead, there was joy. Fun. He made her laugh. He made her live. When Skylar Dawn had joined them, she couldn't imagine anything that might be missing. And now…

"If something happens to her, life won't be possible."

"It'll be okay, dear." Her mother gently patted her back. "I shouldn't have said anything, but I know you'll bring our darling girl home safe and sound."

"You don't know that," Kendall whispered.

She'd been in such control of her future, of her life. Now she was helpless. Absolutely helpless.

Facing her mother, she closed her eyes for a second to strengthen her resolve. Now wasn't the time, but her mother had pushed the issue. When she looked at her mom again, Naomi was crying.

It was totally unexpected. Her mother didn't cry.

Not real tears. She sniffed, stayed stoic and normally didn't show emotion.

"Mother, what's the real reason Dad left?"

Naomi looked taken off guard. "I don't believe that's any of your business. Especially right now."

Kendall didn't want to tell her why the thought had popped into her head. Or that she'd known there would never be an answer. It had been a foolish thirteen-year-old's dream to find him. That hope had long been abandoned.

At first she'd blamed herself, but soon her disappointment had shifted to acceptance. Heath had once asked her why she tolerated so much from her mother. Kendall had never pinpointed the answer until right that minute.

Without her and Skylar Dawn, her mother was alone.

Sitting here, listening to her hatred of Heath… Kendall couldn't take it anymore. No matter what happened, he'd always be Skylar Dawn's daddy. Clearly upset, her mother sniffed then patted her eyes with the tissue again.

"I… I'm sorry, Mother. I really do appreciate all the help you've given us—"

"That's what I'm here for, dear."

"Let me finish." She took her mother's hand between her own. "Because of your anger and bitterness, I almost threw out the best thing that ever happened to me."

"That's not true. *He* left. He walked out on you. And now—"

"I'm sure Heath's going to get your granddaughter back home safely. Like I said…if anything happens to me, Skylar Dawn is his daughter. You might want to rethink how you treat him. I know I am."

"Even if he runs to his mother when things get rough?"

"What are you talking about? Are you saying that you overheard him talking to his mother about us? About our problems?"

"I told you that, dear." The tears were gone as if they'd been calculated the entire time.

She wouldn't have gone that far. Would she? Had she deliberately said the one thing she'd confided that hurt Kendall the most? All these months she'd believed Heath had been confiding in another Ranger and shared their problems with the world instead of her.

"Fair warning, Mother. Things will be changing around here when this is all done. You should begin getting used to that idea."

"It's time to get ready," Heath said from down the hall. "Slate's on his way."

HEATH TAPPED ON their bedroom door, slipped inside and retrieved his suit. Kendall had been right. It wasn't the time to talk. But there would be a discussion when Skylar Dawn came home.

First and most importantly, his focus had to be on his daughter. The kidnapper said he'd have to choose between them. He'd spent the last three hours staring at the ceiling, his head throbbing, his side screaming that he shouldn't move. His mind was caught in a loop that there was no choice.

No man could choose between his wife or daughter. Maybe it would be easier to think about his mother-in-law problem? But that didn't take much thinking. Naomi Barlow didn't believe he was good enough for her daughter. A simple cowboy from a failing Southwest Texas ranch would never be good enough.

A Texas Ranger who loved her daughter and granddaughter more than his own life would never be good enough. Not for her. He couldn't change her mind, and he needed to accept it. If he didn't, he'd lose Kendall.

If he didn't lose her today.

Stubborn and smart, his wife would do everything in her power to return home.

She wanted a promise that he'd do whatever the kidnappers said. He couldn't and wouldn't make that promise to her. He trusted that he'd know what to do when the time came.

He was stubborn and smart, too.

After dressing, he opened the front door and checked on the Rangers from Company F, one in a truck and one on the porch. But the man on the porch wasn't in the traditional suit and tie. Tonight Bryce Johnson was dressed in jeans so he'd blend into the neighborhood.

"Just wanted to let you know that Slate's on his way. I assume no one's been sneaking around or watching the house. You guys need anything?"

"We've got you covered, Heath. Don't mind us," Bryce said, standing and shaking his hand. "You guys were there for Major Parker when the twins were kidnapped. Don't worry about anything here."

"I meant to ask when you got here. How's everyone doing in Waco?"

"We're all good. You let us know if *you* need anything. We're here for you, man." Bryce pumped his hand again, and also clapped him on the shoulder.

"Before I head back in, you got the cell numbers of my team. Right?"

"Wade supplied us with everything we need to keep apprised of the situation. If you need any help, just let us know. Otherwise, I can guarantee you that no one's getting in this house."

This time Heath slapped Bryce on the back. "I don't think we've caught up since that advanced computer stuff in Austin two years ago. We should compare notes again soon."

Bryce nodded.

Heath was ready. At least, he was cleaned up and dressed. He hadn't retrieved his black boots from his closet yet. He rarely wore them, except for special occasions.

He stumbled into the wall, his breath leaving him suddenly. Like he'd been hit again. Skylar Dawn had been kidnapped. He shook himself to regain control. He couldn't lose it. Not now. Not until it was over.

"Are you okay?" Kendall asked. "Do I need to call the doctor?"

Damn, she was beautiful. Dressed and ready to go, with the exception of her shoes. With that dress she should have a smile on her face. Her look of concern seemed out of place—but warranted. He was pretty certain he looked like he needed a doctor.

"No, thanks. I got it." He stood, grabbing his midsection, letting her believe the panic he'd experienced was just his sore ribs. "I got a look at my face, though.

Looks like the beauty will be attending the reception with a beast."

He pointed to the split on his cheekbone held together with Steri-Strips. The bruise around it had already begun to blacken. He tried to joke, but he honestly couldn't have laughed if he tried.

God, he hoped he could do whatever was necessary tonight. *No!* He would push through the pain and get it done, no matter what it took.

"How much did you hear of the conversation with my mother?"

"You were right. This isn't the best time for that particular talk." He stood straight, keeping his breathing as shallow as possible. "Right now, I need to switch to my dress boots. These look weird with this black suit."

"Sit down. I'll get them."

As soon as she left the front hallway, he hobbled to the couch and eased himself onto it. She returned faster than he could move and caught him just as he leaned against the cushions.

"Maybe we should get a stand-in for you."

"That's not happening, Kendall. I'm resting now, but I'd never forgive myself if something happened and I stayed on the sidelines. You know you'd feel the same."

"It was worth a try. But you're right. I would push through all the pain to do my part." She dropped the boots on the floor. "There is one thing I can help with—getting these boots off and the others on."

"I won't let you or Skylar Dawn down, Kendall."

"No matter what happens, I don't and I won't blame you." She slipped the first boot off. "This is the result of my investigation, not yours. It's exactly what I feared most."

"I remember the multiple conversations about not having kids because we both had dangerous jobs. I meant every word back then just as much as you." He caught his breath from the pain as he forgot to brace himself when she tugged the second boot free. "I don't regret the decision to have our daughter, though. No matter what happens."

She took his hand into hers. "Neither do I. Never. And I'm sorry for what Mother implied."

"Later. But while we have a moment—"

"Ding-dong," Slate interrupted, letting himself inside. "How ya doing, partner?"

Heath waved him off. He wouldn't answer every person who asked him that question. Otherwise he'd be reliving the experience every other minute. It was better to concentrate on the task at hand—rescuing Skylar Dawn.

"Did you bring the phones?" Heath asked.

"Phones? We only need the phone he left in the barn." She looked to both men. "What did you have in mind?"

"This guy is probably going to ask you to drop the phone he gave you. Why not drop two that are old and useless?" Slate said.

"That actually makes a lot of sense. I spent some of the time Heath rested moving pictures off this thing." She set her cell on the coffee table. "That's really smart. Thanks, Slate."

"I wish I could take credit. Totally your husband's idea after his was destroyed." He handed her a grocery sack. "Here are your shoes. Best the techs could do quickly."

"I'm still against this idea. It's likely that the kidnapper will have a wand or something."

Heath raised an eyebrow. "Whatever it takes?"

"Right." She slipped both shoes on her feet. "It's worth the try. They may not actually be as smart as us."

"So what we did is clone your phones." Slate pointed to the two older versions. "If the kidnappers call your number instead of the phone they left, we'll still be covered. And just in case they allow you to keep the phones, we have you covered with a tracker. Reception begins at seven. Are you guys ready?"

"Give us a minute."

"Sure, man. I'll be in the van."

Heath waited for the door to click closed. He pulled both boots almost all the way on, then stood, slipping them on the rest of the way. When he was done, Kendall threw her arms around his shoulders.

"No matter what—" she kissed his cheek "—I love you and Skylar Dawn more than anything in my life. You two are the most important things in my life. The best things that ever happened to me."

"You took the words right from my heart."

Chapter Nineteen

"Want to dance?" Heath asked her to ease the tension between not only everyone watching them, but the two of them. With his injuries he could only sway. Kendall gently wrapped her arms around his neck. Maybe they'd have a moment to finish talking about the thoughts that had run through his head while he'd been in the living room and van.

"Dammit, Heath, you can't take off like that," Slate said from behind him.

They both ignored him. Kendall drew a deep breath and said, "I need to say something."

He looked at her seeing no one else. Beautiful eyes filled with tears but didn't overflow. Then she blinked them away.

"I'm sorry."

"What?" He was confused. Why would she be sorry? He's the one who lost their daughter.

"Before you moved out, Mother told me she overheard you talking about our problems on the phone. I was angry you'd talk with someone else and not a counselor."

"Just Mom."

"I realize that now. I should have known."

"I should have told you."

They swayed into the middle of the temporary dance floor at a wedding reception they weren't supposed to be attending. Thinking about wedding vows really hit him in a vulnerable place. No way would he admit that to anyone. But the reminder did its job. Who was he to decide which of their careers was more important?

If she'd have him…he would move to Portland. He bent his head, kissing her neck sweetly, just to remind her he was there. She tilted her face, her eyes closed. For a moment he forgot where they were as his lips softly captured hers. He meant it as a comforting kiss, almost a farewell in case something happened to them.

But Kendall changed it. She kissed him longingly and then drew away, breathless. His body was on fire from the brief encounter.

"You shouldn't kiss me like that," he said into her hair.

"Uh-huh," she mumbled with her head on his shoulder, her breath softly caressing the small hairs on his neck.

"I wish Skylar Dawn was safely at home. Then I could spin you around the dance floor until we forgot all our problems," Heath whispered in her ear. He turned and brought her body closer still, holding the small of her back firmly under his hands.

"I don't need a dance floor to forget," she said, barely loud enough for him to hear. "I want to be a family again, Heath."

A tap on his shoulder stopped his reply. Slate interrupted, handing him a cell phone.

"It's on mute. But this is our guy. He called me instead of the burner or either of you. He knew it would take us longer to get a lock on him."

They all moved off the dance floor. Slate tactfully blocked anyone from approaching so he could answer the call in semi-private.

"This is Murray."

"Drop your phones in the lobby fountain. A cab's waiting for you. You have four minutes to be at the northwest corner of Elm and Houston. Don't speak or signal the others with you at the reception. Keep the line open, Ranger Murray. You don't want to endanger your daughter."

"Where do we go?"

"I don't repeat myself, Ranger. Take this phone with you and don't disconnect. I'll be monitoring your progress to verify you're following my instructions. Drop your cells in the large fountain on your way out the door. You have four minutes."

The line went silent. Heath was careful not to push the end button. He grabbed Kendall's hand and pulled her toward the lobby.

"That was him?"

"Yeah. We have four minutes to get to Elm and Houston." He dropped the old cell Slate had given him into the fountain. Kendall took her fake phone from her clutch purse and did the same.

"Where are you going?"

He pushed through the revolving door and asked the doorman, "Do you have a cab waiting?"

"I have one for Heath and Kendall."

"That's us." Heath turned to her, pointing to the cell screen to show that the call was still active. "We agreed to do everything exactly as he said. We have four minutes to get there." He put his arm around her, tugging her close. "We might make it if we're lucky."

"One swipe with a wand and the shoes are blown," she whispered close to his ear in order not to be picked up by the phone.

"The guy told me Elm and Houston," the driver said. "Any particular corner?"

"Northwest. There's extra if you get us there in three minutes," Heath told the driver.

"No problem if you let me drop you. The actual corner requires me to circle 'round."

"Fine. Why did he give us only four minutes to get there?" he asked softly. He dropped a twenty on the front seat.

"He had to be watching us. Now we don't have time to contact any of the agencies watching us." Her eyes went to the cell in his hand.

"He told me not to disconnect." He listened to the phone. "Nothing. He's listening and keeping us from contacting anyone."

"He'll probably have another cell waiting for us. We'll jump to another location. He'll try to lose our tail before we can do anything about it. Did you recognize his voice? Could it be Marrone? A high-paid lawyer got him released."

"No, it was the same guy as this morning, but not Marrone."

In a louder voice Kendall asked the cab driver, "How far are we?"

"Just two more turns. You sure are in a hurry to see the grassy knoll."

"The grassy knoll?" they both asked.

"Yeah, man. Elm and Houston is where Kennedy got shot," said the cab driver.

"I didn't recognize the street names." Kendall pressed her fingers to her temple. "That means people, as in tourists."

"Very good, Ranger," said a distant voice and Heath brought Slate's phone to his ear again. "Continue on Elm. The phone's under the tracks. Don't forget to leave your partner's cell in the cab."

"This is going to sound strange, but we need to continue on Elm and be dropped on the other side of the rail overpass," Heath repeated to the cab driver.

"I can't stop there, man. It's a blind curve." The cabby stuck out his hand waiting for extra cash.

"Pull up on the sidewalk," Kendall told him. They left the cab and the phone. "What else did he say?"

The sky was clear, and he could see a few of the brightest stars in the sky. They crossed the dangerous street as fast as they could. Their four minutes were up.

"Hey!" a man shouted from the opposite side of six lanes. "Are you Heath and Kendall?"

"Yes!" they shouted across the busy six lanes of traffic.

"This guy on the phone said to head for the stairs back there." He lowered a cell onto the ledge and pointed toward the way they had come. "Damn. I'm calling the cops. That guy said he'd kill me if I didn't yell for you."

Avoiding oncoming traffic, they moved further into the underpass and ran across Commerce and Elm streets.

"Good grief, the stench." Kendall covered her nose with her hand.

"It smells like a hundred elephants from the circus relieved themselves."

"I can't believe you're making jokes."

"I thought I was being factual." He guided her along the narrow sidewalk toward the cell.

"We're sitting ducks, you know. The kidnapper has cut us off from our backup with all these one-way streets. We're on a dark walkway that might as well be a tunnel. The car trailing us passed without ever slowing down. We can't be sure they saw us at all."

They exited the semi-tunnel. How many times had he driven through here and not taken a serious look. They both drew clean air deep into their lungs. Heath searched Dealy Plaza on the edge of the city of Dallas. Very few people walked the sidewalks, but the kidnapper could be any one of them.

"How long 'til they realize we're not in the cab?" she asked.

"Until the cab stops for the FBI. Slate will be trailing your shoes. They'll hang back long enough to make it look like they lost us."

The phone rang as they approached the ledge, making it easy to find.

"Walk north through the parking lot, turn east, cross Houston Street, and follow the light rail on Pacific Avenue. Make your way to the West End Marketplace. Don't borrow any phone along the way, Murray. We're watching."

"This way." Heath guided Kendall past a picket fence to the parking lot for the Kennedy Museum.

Mental pictures of President Kennedy's assassination invaded his thoughts. If the kidnapper wanted to give them a feeling of doom, he'd succeeded.

"He more than likely is watching us. What now?" she asked.

"We're to go to the West End."

They began the trek, following the kidnapper's instructions. The light rail street was closed to cars and had no pedestrians.

"At least he can't hear us now," Heath said.

"You hope." She nodded toward the phone. "Try that yet?"

"Password protected. I can answer, but can't dial."

"Figures." Kendall stepped around a shattered beer bottle. She grabbed his hand, causing him to stop and look at her. "Remember your promise to let me handle the kidnapper. You get Skylar Dawn to safety. That's the only thing you need to do."

His tug on her hand got her walking again. "That dress is beautiful. I haven't seen you wear that since we had a night out three years ago. Wow. It's really been that long?"

At his change of subject, she dropped his hand. "You promised, Heath."

"Not exactly. I told you I wouldn't choose. Let's get there and find Skylar Dawn."

He caught her hand in his, seeking anyone out of the ordinary. People walked in both directions. It was a beautiful spring evening to be strolling the West End. And it seemed like everyone was.

They rounded a corner onto Market Street, which was full of people. They headed toward an open courtyard where a band played. The phone rang, slicing through the dull roar of the street noise. Before he could pull it from his pocket, Kendall stepped in front of him.

"There is no choice, Heath. Skylar Dawn needs you. I know how to handle this creep. Leave him to me."

Keeping his eyes on her face, he brought the phone to his ear as it rang. "Yeah?"

"It is time to choose, Ranger. Your wife or your child."

"Where's Skylar Dawn?"

"She'll be safe for twenty more minutes."

"Damn it, man! What do you want?"

"Your wife. I can see you both. Send her to the Dallas Aquarium. I'll call again to tell you where the girl is when I have your wife."

The line went dead.

"Did he say where Skylar Dawn is?"

He shook his head, frustration keeping him momentarily silent. "I'm supposed to stay here, wait for his call. He'll let me know where to pick up Skylar Dawn after he has you."

"Don't worry about me, Heath. I'm trusting you to find our daughter."

"He wants you to start walking toward the aquarium," he said, pointing behind her toward the building.

They'd taken Skylar Dawn there several times. Seeing the endangered animals section was her second favorite thing to do. The first was riding Stardust.

"You can do this." She squeezed his hand, pushing the phone to his chest.

"I'm not worried about me. He's…"

There wasn't enough time to explain what he wanted her to know. He should have answered her before they left the dance floor. She was walking straight into the hands of a madman, with a strong possibility they'd never see each other again.

"Come back to me, Kendall."

She turned to walk away, but he caught her off guard and pulled her into his arms. His lips claimed hers with the hunger of a starving man, the desperation of a defeated one. He'd never known a kiss so transparent. He'd never experienced a kiss filled with regret and longing. Regret for what might have been and longing for what might never be.

His wife pulled slowly away, her free hand cupping his cheek.

"I wish you had a gun or I could send backup. Something." His voice rose in frustration. "I can't just let you turn yourself over to him."

"He's watching. I've got to go, Heath. Find our girl."

She lifted his fingers from her arm and kissed him one last time. Then she put one foot in front of the other and walked away from him. Stopping himself from following was pretty much the hardest thing he'd done in his life.

Chapter Twenty

Heath stood there until she was out of sight. He shoved the phone in his back pocket then ran into the crowd gathered and enjoying a night out. A couple walked toward him and he didn't hesitate—no matter what the kidnapper had insinuated earlier.

"Excuse me, do you have a cell phone? This is an emergency. My daughter is missing."

"Oh my God. Here," the woman said as she handed him her phone.

"I can't tell you how much I appreciate this. Could we walk?" He didn't wait on an answer. Just turned and heard them follow. He dialed Wade's number on the woman's phone. "Come on, pick up," he murmured.

Continuing to move, he ignored the man trying to sell him a bouquet and hit End. He punched the number again. The couple continued to follow.

"Heath? Kendall?"

"The kidnapper split us up. He sent Kendall to the aquarium," he shouted into the phone, looking at the people around him. "Once he has her, he's calling a burner with my daughter's location. Get to the aquarium. Fast. I'll meet you there."

"Where are—"

He heard part of Wade's shout as he clicked the phone off.

"Thanks for your help." The phone was barely back in the stranger's hand before he pushed his way through the crowd, running to find his wife.

But she was gone. No bright red dress anywhere.

Nervous energy kept him running toward the aquarium. A van pulled up next to him.

"Get in!" Slate yelled. "We're tracking Kendall. She's already heading north."

Heath jumped with his three friends and fellow Rangers. Then Slate pulled back into traffic. They were a block away from where he'd been told to stay before he suddenly remembered the phone in his back pocket needed to stay put on that corner. "Pull over." Heath waved the phone at his partners.

"What? Why?" the three Rangers shouted.

"Hell, he's probably tracking you through that thing," Wade said, taking it from his hand.

"Once he has Kendall, he said he'd call and tell me where Skylar Dawn is."

"Who do we go after? It's totally your call, man. Jerry Fisher is standing by, along with a host of other FBI agents. Then we've got the Dallas PD. The other Company B Rangers are posted around the city," Jack said.

"Whichever you choose, I'm with you. I'm your partner. We've got your back," Slate confirmed.

They wouldn't try to change his mind. Not about staying with him to find his daughter and not about chasing after Kendall. The team would do whatever he asked.

"I can stay here, wait on the call. That way the tracker doesn't move," Jack suggested from the front seat.

"You might want this." Wade handed Heath an earpiece communication device, a cell phone and a Glock.

"I can't do this. I can't choose." Heath was torn.

Wade looked at the tracker. "We've got a few minutes before we know where he's sent Kendall. But we don't know what hoops he's going to make her jump through. I don't know if the tracker will remain intact. She might even ditch it herself. She was against it to begin with."

Kendall wanted him to rescue Skylar Dawn. He had to rescue them both. One without the other was still failure. How would his daughter ever forgive him if he let something happen to her mother? The Rangers didn't do failure.

Wade rested his hand on his shoulder. "What do you want us to do?"

"We're going after Kendall." He looked straight at Slate, handing him the phone. "I'm trusting you with my daughter's life."

"I won't let you down."

Thirteen minutes later they'd followed the tracker to the Galleria Mall. Slate had stayed behind with a plan to forward the call and for Heath to speak to the kidnappers himself. Then they wouldn't know he was closer to them than they'd hoped.

Wade dropped Jack, then he drove to the opposite end of the mall to drop Heath. The phone he'd given to Heath rang.

A text from Slate stated the company phone was set with the forwarded call and he should just answer it.

"Murray."

"Kendall has arrived, and I'm a man of my word. Your little girl loves roses as much as you do."

The phone disconnected.

"What happened? Where is she?" Heath yelled.

The phone rang again. "It's Slate. Do you know what he's talking about?"

"It…it has to be the house on Vandelia Street off Wycliff, where I caught Saundra Rosa. It has bloodred roses on the south side. Orange trim around the windows and doors."

"I'm closer. I'll take a police unit with me," Slate let them know.

"I should be there."

"Kendall needs you. I'll get Skylar Dawn. You can count on me."

Silence. Wade waited to move.

"The bastard didn't give any instructions. His real target has always been Kendall, just like we thought." Had he done the right thing?

"Let's go get her." Wade faced forward and put the van in gear.

Heath slammed the panel door and ran. He hoped and prayed his wife would forgive him for coming after her and leaving Skylar Dawn's rescue to another Ranger.

KENDALL STOPPED AT the mall entrance and threw her shoes in the trash. She didn't want to jeopardize anything by letting the Rangers rescue her before she had her daughter's location.

The private car had obviously been sent by the kidnappers. She'd been locked in. No borrowing the driver's phone or talking to him. After the car arrived, the driver had stood at his door to watch her go inside. He'd simply stated that her party would be on the fourth floor.

They knew she was here.

But so did the Rangers.

Now if she could just find another way to let them follow her. The only thing she had in her clutch was that tube of Cherry Bomb red lipstick and two five-dollar bills. She'd refused any fancy gadgets except the tracker in her shoes.

Barefoot and in a tight, short dress, there weren't too many options left. No bread crumbs to leave behind. She leaned on a post on the way to the escalators. Maybe there was something…

Taking the lipstick, she drew a thick *H* on her heel. *H* for Heath. It was worth a shot.

At the bottom of each level of escalators, she left a Cherry Bomb *H*. At the top she'd limp to a bench, discretely reapply the lipstick and then limp to the next up escalator. When she pressed her heel, she left a red spot at each level.

Once on the fourth level, she reapplied and waited on the bench. Good thing she sat down. Her insides were jumping around, making her glad she hadn't eaten. What if Skylar Dawn hadn't eaten? She had to focus, be confident. The Rangers would rescue their daughter. Heath had promised. He never lied. Bringing down the kidnapper was her job. She could do this.

Please, Heath, find our baby.

Chapter Twenty-One

"Special Agent Barlow, you've lost your shoes. And you're limping."

When she turned her head, following the familiar voice, she had a moment of pure rage at his release from custody. The man who'd turned her life into a shambles sat beside her like her best friend. The gun sticking in her ribs came as little surprise.

"Bryan Marrone. Public Exposure sent their favorite lackey, I see. I guess I shouldn't have believed you were innocent yesterday." She didn't explain why she was barefoot. Maybe he hadn't seen her with the lipstick.

"True, Kendall. It didn't take much to avoid the cops and kill Saundra. She was a sweet kid, but enough with the pink already. I prefer a lady in red any day."

"I'll put you in jail this time and throw away the key. Where is my little girl? This was supposed to be an exchange of me for her. If anything's happened to her I'll—"

"Stop being so damn dramatic." He poked the gun into her ribs until she began moving to the side of the escalators. His jacket hung over his arm, hiding the gun. To onlookers, he looked like a polite escort with his hand on her back.

"Where's Skylar Dawn?"

"I told your husband." He pushed her toward an alcove. "Don't worry about her. Do as I say and nothing will happen."

"You phoned Heath? Is she here at the mall?" Why didn't Heath recognize this man's voice? "What do you get out of this? Who's in on this with you?"

"Do you actually expect me to tell you everything? I'm not stupid, Kendall. Move to your left. I need to pat you down."

Kendall moved as slowly as she could. The lipstick on her heel smeared a little on the floor. He yanked up her foot, looking at the light trail behind them.

"Dammit, Kendall." He snatched the lipstick from her purse and tossed it into the throng of people, then yanked her out of the group of shoppers. "Show me the bottom of your foot. Your attempt to leave a trail might really get you killed. Do you have any electronic devices that are going to make me angrier?"

"Of course not. We didn't have time." But she did have the side of her other foot. *Thank God.*

"And I'm supposed to believe you?" He rubbed his hands up and down her body. "You know, ever since you rubbed my leg I wanted to return the favor."

The shiver that crept up her spine was accompanied by acid from her stomach. Marrone's hands lingered over her breasts and hips. Her stomach soured more… if that was possible.

"Oh, wait. Our modern times make detecting electronic devices easy. Put your hands on your head."

There, in plain sight of dozens of people, he pulled an EMF detector from a backpack and waved the wand close to her body. He smiled and made lewd gestures at a couple of men, who snapped a picture or video.

"I knew you were a smart woman. You wouldn't do anything to jeopardize your daughter. Wipe your foot off. You sure you wouldn't prefer money over the cowboy?"

"Give me my daughter."

He'd made a mistake. One of these people would surely post something to social media. That would help prosecute him. But more importantly, if he made one mistake, he'd make another. That's when she'd make her move, but she needed him to reveal where they were holding Skylar Dawn.

"Head toward the service hall. That way." He shoved her to a back entrance to some of the shops.

Kendall tried to think of ways to stall for time. Surely the Rangers had followed her, but there was no guarantee.

"What did you do with my daughter?"

"Your daughter is safer than you. Those freaks may be weird, but they aren't going to hurt a kid. It'll take some time for the Rangers to determine her whereabouts. Too bad the top brass wanted you out of the picture. I could have saved the day, been a real hero."

Skylar Dawn was okay? Not in danger? Before entering the service hallway, she spun to face him. "You know, every single time a creep on the other side of the table claims they do it for the money, it makes no sense to me. Please tell me there's more to this. Some great cause or reason."

"There's a cause. Huge cause. But you wouldn't understand." He jammed her side once again. She couldn't defend herself against the gun when it was this close. "Turn and walk, or I'll pull the trigger in spite of how long Brantley Lourdes wants this to last. Of course it's about the money."

"Public Exposure is paying you to keep me away from the investigation, and you don't really know anything?"

Another jab. Another sharp pain. "Walk."

His cool, unhurried attitude worried her. Did he really think she came alone? Why didn't *he* think that the Rangers would be here any minute?

HEATH SLAMMED THE entrance door into the wall and instantly drew the attention of everyone entering or exiting the high-end mall. "Damn. Sorry."

"Your wife tossed her shoes in the trash can," Wade said. "Just like we thought she would. They haven't moved since we arrived."

Where would she be? It had taken three minutes after the tracker stopped for the kidnapper to spot Kendall before he called back with his cryptic message. That was the only clue they had. Skylar Dawn better be at that house.

"Where would he try to take her?" he mumbled, but his earpiece picked it up.

"We've got the closest exits to where she entered covered," Jack said.

"There's too many of them. We need more units," Wade added.

"No. Units outside might put her in jeopardy. Kendall's smart. Look for something. Listen for anything unusual," Heath told them.

The place was packed. Heath searched for a bright red dress on his way, but didn't see one. Lots of dresses, lots of suits, hats, boots, tennis shoes, shorts…but no bright red dress or bare feet.

Maybe he could see from the top. Before he went to the next floor, he had to stop and catch his breath. *Damn ribs.* He leaned on a pole, his eyes scanning for someone with no shoes. There on the floor was an *H*. He bent and wiped the mark. Lipstick.

How many random *H*'s would be on the floor of a packed mall? It had to be Kendall. She'd left a trail of bread crumbs…or red lipstick, in this case.

Several minutes behind her, he rushed as much as he could without pushing people out of his way. If Kendall's trail played out, he might be able to catch up. He looked above his head, barely able to see the escalators to the next floor.

"Stall, Kendall. Stall."

Heath followed the *H* marks at the bottom of each escalator. On the fourth floor, the lipstick led to the hallway with the elevators. "I'm on her trail, near the ice rink elevators. No doubts. I just don't know how far ahead they are."

After he punched the down button again, he slammed his fist into his hand, wishing he were hitting the maniac who had Kendall or Skylar Dawn. The thought of losing either of them forever propelled Heath on. He punched every button, tapping the wall, waiting for the doors to open, checking each floor for her now smeared lipstick mark.

By now they should have police units ready to move in. Hopefully. Except…there was a hotel and bar near taxis or ride-share pickups. Dammit. That was how this guy would leave. "Guys? He's heading for the hotel."

"Are you sure?" both asked.

"Yeah. There's no way he'd use his own vehicle. He's got Kendall for insurance, but he's already admitted he doesn't have Skylar Dawn."

There was no time to wait. The lipstick imprint had been getting fainter.

"YOU SEEM LIKE a smart guy, Marrone." Kendall slowed her pace again until he shoved her forward. "How in the world did you get mixed up with Public Exposure?"

Marrone yanked her around a corner. "Money. Lots of money. There really isn't any other reason. Some of those people are 'true believers'. Freaks. Just remember—I will pull this trigger. I can get away while they're trying to keep you alive."

"We could stop right now, if you'd like." The light quip accompanied by a forced smile took control to deliver. The horrifying hatred in his eyes didn't have her feeling lighthearted or in control.

Leaving the elevator, he gestured toward the men's restroom. Ahead of them, Kendall could hear the sounds of loud music and people. A bar? It should be packed at this time of night. The wheels turned furiously in her mind. The small bathroom space was empty except for one man washing his hands. He left, giving Marrone a sly smile.

"Should I call you Marrone? *Perp*, *kidnapper* or *suspect* probably won't go over too well in public."

"Neither would blowing a hole in your gut." He leaned on the door. "I noticed you limping slightly. Heath give that to you while dancing?" he asked with a smirk.

"I'll be fine." She wasn't actually limping, but she wasn't about to correct the jerk. Rolling to the side of her foot, she occasionally left a mark of lipstick. It was her only hope that someone could follow them.

She wanted to scream at him to stop this stupid charade and tell her Skylar Dawn's location. The longing to see her baby girl again wouldn't allow her to lose it. Instead, she needed to get him talking, bragging, something to give her a clue where her daughter had been taken. Or what other men were involved.

"Well, you won't be feeling any pain in a few hours. You'll already be dead when people discover what Public Exposure is really up to. Before they bring Dallas to its knees with the destruction and mass casualties." He said it coldly, with no emotion, as if killing people was an everyday occurrence.

Kendall knew he spoke the truth...and believed it. "Just tell me where Skylar Dawn is. You can go. I won't say anything to Heath or anyone else."

"In the last stall you'll find some clothing. Please leave the door open and change." He made a grand gesture like a butler, then backed up against the door again to keep others out.

The sloppy T-shirt wasn't too bad. The overalls were very large and made moving her legs difficult. The dirty-blond wig needed a good shampoo and brushing. She left the cherry-red dress on the stall door. As she emerged, he dangled a pair of handcuffs in one hand.

"Are the cuffs really necessary?"

He tossed them at her. She felt like an idiot snapping them on herself.

"Most definitely. Consider it payback." He pulled a small sweater from his pack. "Cover the handcuffs. I wouldn't want to alarm any of the patrons."

The door opened and she stumbled as he pushed her through. Angry enough to take off his head, she had to calm down and think. She had to stop him before he could escape. She couldn't trust he told Heath the truth. If he hadn't they may never find their daughter.

The hotel bar was crowded and dark. People were squished together, attempting to get from one side of the bar to the other. It slowed their progression, giving her a chance to work on Marrone.

"You should be in a hurry," she said, attempting to sound completely confident. "The Texas Rangers are probably hot on our trail."

The loud music didn't drown his demonic laugh. Kendall wouldn't allow it to upset her. She used it to strengthen her resolve instead. This was the last time the creep would harm anyone.

Before he shoved her into another person to get her walking again, she made her move. She waved, then shouted, "Over here!"

He snatched her wrist from the air.

Pulling him forward, she kneed his groin hard enough to make the manliest of men cry. As he doubled over, she brought her knee up under his chin, throwing his head backward. His arm tangled in the links of the cuffs and caused him to bring her to the floor with him.

Several people cushioned their fall. Everything in

the bar ground to a halt. She tried to push him from her, but he brought her hand across her throat, pressing the metal against her windpipe. By grasping the cuffs, he successfully held her, and then hit her temple with the butt of the gun.

With an excited smile forming on his thin lips, he pressed the barrel next to her ear. "That wasn't very nice, Kendall. Come with me or I open fire."

Still dazed, she allowed him to pull her to her feet. She splayed her hands and warned the men approaching, "Stay back. He'll shoot you. Stay back."

"Let the lady go!"

They both crashed back to the floor. She hadn't gotten a look at what—or who—had hit them. Through a fog, she saw a man in a black suit lift Marrone off her and raise his fist.

Heath. He'd found her. Thank God for Cherry Bomb red lipstick. He landed his punch, sending Marrone crashing into a table.

Wait! Why was Heath here? The music still blared and the lights from the dance floor flashed, but most of the women were watching Heath.

She didn't blame them. She liked watching him, too. The attempt at standing didn't work well. She settled for leaning on an elbow and watching her husband work.

"Did they find Skylar Dawn? Where's the gun? It must have gone flying."

"You okay?" he asked her.

Heath lifted Marrone by his shirt collar but let him crumple back to the floor. Heath knelt and frisked him. "He's out cold. No keys. Just a cell phone."

"We got him covered for you," a man with the bar's

logo on his T-shirt said. "He ain't going anywhere. Look after your girlfriend."

"Wife." Heath yanked Marrone's backpack off finding nothing of importance.

"You sure did give him what for," someone said, slapping him on the back.

Another man with the bar's logo rolled Marrone face-down and cuffed his hands behind his back. "I knew these would come in handy one day." He grinned. "I called the cops."

Heath flipped Marrone's phone open. "Dammit. Needs a password."

"Nice flying tackle, man. She need an ambulance?" the bartender asked, pointing to Kendall.

"Can you sit up? You okay, honey?" He helped her lean against him. "Helluva stall there, Kendall. Your eye's already swelling."

"You haven't answered me, Heath. You were supposed to get our daughter. Did you find her? Is she safe?"

All the adrenaline left her body with just his look. His rescuing of her would mean nothing without their daughter. Panic pulled her fully to her senses.

"Oh my God. Wake him up and do whatever's necessary to him. We have to find out where they've taken her."

Security guards entered the bar. "Everyone stay where you are."

"He gave us a clue. Slate's heading there along with Jason's DPD units. We should know any minute. Just rest and I'll get us out of here." He kissed her quickly and stood.

"You should have gone for her."

"I'll explain later." He grabbed his broken ribs and sucked air through his teeth, hissing.

But he wasn't the snake. Brantley Lourdes and all of Public Exposure were the cold-blooded creatures who had taken their little girl.

"We're going to be a family again, Kendall. I didn't get to answer you before. Take the transfer to Portland. If that's what you want…then go for it. I'll come with you and stay home with Skylar Dawn until she's okay. We'll figure out how to do this."

Chapter Twenty-Two

Heath handed the phone to Kendall. The next phone call would be the most important of his life. The seconds ticked by as they waited. Wade arrived and then Jack, who swiped on his phone as he came through the bar door.

"Major Clements hasn't heard anything either," Jack said.

The phone rang with an old-fashioned bell. Heath froze. They all did except Kendall. She answered and immediately switched to speaker.

"I've got her. Skylar Dawn is safe and unharmed."

He heard the words and sank to the floor next to Kendall. No matter what their status—separated, together or moving—they were both her parents.

"Man, that was intense," Wade said, relieving a little of the tension.

Heath helped Kendall to her feet. "Let's go get our daughter." Then he looked at Wade and stuck out his hand.

"Here's your badge. I thought you might need it." Wade placed it in Heath's palm.

Then Jack nudged Wade. "Keys. He's waiting for

our ride. But it might be faster if you bring it around to the bar's outdoor entrance. In their shape, it might take them an hour to walk to wherever you parked."

"Good idea," Heath and Kendall both answered.

"Let me get you some ice." Jack headed behind the bar to the men who had helped earlier.

"Your eye's going to be spectacular."

"Why did you come after me, Heath? You were supposed to save Skylar Dawn."

"We did save her. I told you I wouldn't choose. I accepted a plan that worked to save you both."

"What if it hadn't worked?" Kendall's eyes filled with tears.

He wanted to hold her, not debate his decision. He'd argued with himself every step of the way to finding her. What if this…what if that…

"I won't argue about it. You're both safe. That's the only outcome I need to think about."

Jack gave her a bar towel full of ice for the side of her head. Kendall was in good hands. Heath walked away, straight through the outer doors to wait on the sidewalk. Now wasn't the time to disagree. He needed air. He showed his badge and found the Dallas PD.

"A white panel van is on its way to pick me up. Can you make sure someone lets it into the drop-off circle? Thanks."

He was resting on a short cement barrier, when a set of very lovely arms wrapped around his chest.

"I'm sorry." She kissed his neck. "And I'm grateful." She kissed the other side of his neck then moved around to look him in the eye. "And you're right." She took his hand between her own. "We're safe. That's all that matters."

Jack joined them and Wade pulled around. The minutes seemed like hours until the van pulled onto Vandelia Street. Kendall jumped out, meeting Slate for the handoff. Heath moved a little slower, but was right there in time to answer Skylar Dawn's questions.

"I lost my hat, Daddy."

"Mommy found it, baby. It's okay."

"That mean man didn't hurt Stardust, did he?"

"Nope. She's safe and sound with her momma. Just like you." He kissed her forehead. "Let's go home."

"Can we go to McDonald's first? All those people had were carrot sticks."

"Sure, baby, we can do that. Let's go home."

"OH, MY DARLINGS. I can't believe everything turned out okay," Naomi said as they came through the door. She hugged them all. Even Heath. "She is okay, right?"

"Maybe a little dirty and in the same clothes, but she's fine." Heath wouldn't let his mother-in-law take his girl from his arms.

"I'll run a bath." Naomi ran from the room, a tissue covering her mouth.

"I'm not telling her to leave tonight."

"I didn't ask you to. It's safer if she stays here, with the watchdogs out front."

"What do you think?" Kendall asked, looking away from the Rangers' unmarked cars sitting in front of the house.

"We can rest easy. No one's getting through all the Texas Rangers parked around this house."

"No, I meant…" She gently lifted a strand of hair from Skylar Dawn's face and looped it around a cute little ear.

"We've both had the training, sweetheart," he whispered. "You know that we need to find her a good counselor, talk this out, answer her questions. But from what she's said, they dropped her off at that house and she played."

They caved and let Naomi give her a bath, parking themselves at the open door. Skylar Dawn had lots of bubbles to play with. His mother-in-law would have a mess to clean up, but no one cared.

"I keep going over what Marrone said." Kendall backed up to his chest and lifted her mouth so he could hear her lowered voice. "I thought at the time, this was all a plan to get me out of the picture."

"That was my first thought when he gave me the location to pick our girl up."

"Whatever Public Exposure has been working on, it's happening soon. Marrone said there would be mass casualties. I need to talk with him."

"Call Jerry. Let him handle it. She needs us both right now."

She looped her arms carefully around his neck. "I need you both, too. Maybe you should shower while I get her dried off and dressed for bed."

A breath separated their faces. He wanted to kiss her. He shouldn't kiss her. He was dying to kiss her.

He kissed her.

And she definitely kissed him back.

The perfect fit. The perfect taste. He slipped into the memory of her in his arms, in a sexy sparkly dress with a strap that didn't want to stay on her shoulder. He'd wanted to kiss her from the moment their eyes had met. Even on an investigation, he hadn't waited long. Before the week's end, they were in each other's arms, close enough to melt into the other's soul.

Tonight was no different. It was as if the years had all slipped away last night. His body felt alive again, on fire. He wanted her badly enough that it ached.

A caress across his face slipped down to his shoulders and pressed him away. But his last intention was to stop. They had been close to losing everything. He needed more of her, craved more from her lips. Desire was like an infection in his blood, surging with every pulsing beat of his heart.

But a small giggle from Skylar Dawn reined in his longing. She was laughing at them. They drifted slightly apart, then he lifted her between them.

"I'll only be a minute."

He laid loud, sloppy kisses on both their foreheads and transferred their daughter to his wife. No matter what...they were a family.

KENDALL USED A giant fluffy towel to cover Skylar Dawn. She put her in pink pj's and braided her hair after brushing it. By the time she was finished, Heath was done and had collected *The Wizard of Oz* from the living room where they'd left it.

She heard Heath begin reading and jumped in the shower. He'd taken a cloth and a bottle of water, then washed her feet clean while they'd waited on transport home.

Scrubbing hard, she scoured every place the filthy

Bryan Marrone had touched her, then tossed the exfo-
liating sponge in the trash. Maybe it was a good thing
they wouldn't see him tonight. She might tear his head
off for what he'd done.

Tomorrow was soon enough.

She dressed and braided her own hair before slipping
into bed with the loves of her life. Then the what-ifs
began. Heath's arm was around Skylar Dawn, and he
slipped his fingers through hers.

"You can't do that to yourself," Heath whispered.
"No one's to blame. We're good. All safe and sound."

How did he even know she blamed herself? Maybe
because he'd already had time to do the same?

"It's no one's fault. I…"

"Kendall," he squeezed her hand, "we deal with this
tomorrow. Not tonight. Maybe for a while we can just
forget."

"You're right," she said, staring at the ceiling.

"Again?" He laughed softly. "This being right thing
goes straight to my head. I think I like it."

"Shh, you'll wake the baby." She used her free hand
to tuck the light blanket around her little girl's shoulders.

"She's not such a baby anymore," Heath whispered
again. "Her birthday's just around the corner. Get some
sleep."

He turned off the headboard lamp. She closed her
eyes and tried—really tried—to sleep. It didn't work.
She switched on the HISTORY channel, clicked the
mute button and tried again. She was still wide awake.

The TV glowed, casting eerie shadows over the garment bag. It hung over the chair Heath had sat in only

last night. She rolled to her back, stretching muscles she'd forgotten she had.

The room suddenly went dark. She swallowed the moment of blind panic, preparing for an attack.

It took a minute for her to realize she'd moved against the remote, clicking the off button. She wished she could laugh. There was no immediate threat, but for a split second, terror—a too-familiar and unwelcome emotion—had suppressed her intelligence. She cautiously moved from under the covers.

Public Exposure would make a move soon. She hated not doing anything, but their daughter needed them. Needed to know that she was safe.

But was she? Public Exposure was still out there. Planning.

Was anyone safe? Was Marrone telling the truth about a catastrophe? If he was, there weren't many hours left to get the details from him. Who was working on it? Would he talk to them? She should be there, watching the interrogation. It might trigger something she'd forgotten.

Kendall couldn't sleep. She tried to place bits of information into logical categories in her mind. But her mind had other plans. It kept burning the image of Heath's face on the backs of her eyelids.

The image of him smiling as he got on one knee and proposed. He really was gorgeous. Possibly the most handsome man she'd ever met. Her cowboy. It didn't seem possible he could have grown more handsome, but he had.

Some of the cockiness she'd noticed during their first assignment together was gone. Strange how she missed it. Maybe not strange, since she hadn't thought about working with him in years. But he was much more than that. Even though she'd withheld answers, he'd accepted and offered his help.

Skylar Dawn was so much like him. She had his eyes, his thick hair and that cute little attitude when she slipped on a pair of Western boots. Even the way she stubbornly held her mouth. On Heath it was sexy. But on her darling little girl, it had always been a constant reminder of who her father was.

God, she missed being a real family.

Before she'd met Heath, the closest she'd gotten to settling down was having the same apartment for more than six months. Her mother had encouraged her every step of the way, and she'd accepted the help. But the looks her mom had been sending Heath's way this week were wrong. It was time for Naomi Barlow to accept her son-in-law.

If she wanted her life back—and she did—Heath and her daughter had to come first. She just couldn't imagine life without Skylar Dawn. And the past six months proved life without Heath wasn't a life either. She'd been simply existing. Not living.

In order to protect them both, so they could get on with living properly, she couldn't dwell on what their future *might* be. She needed to determine who had attempted to kill her…and why. Then catch the bastard before he succeeded.

They had a life to live.

Chapter Twenty-Three

Giggles and the smell of strong coffee awoke Kendall—
followed by her daughter's attempt to sneak back into
bed. Then came lots more giggles and a few shushes
from Heath.

"Ready?" her husband whispered. "One. Two. Three."

"Surprise!" Skylar Dawn shouted in her sweet voice.
"Wake up, Mommy. We made toast and omelets."

"Oh my goodness." Kendall pushed pillows behind
to prop herself up.

Heath set the tray across her lap, immediately moving
the hot coffee to her bedside table. Skylar Dawn twisted
around on her knees, grabbed Heath's pillow and carefully plumped it behind her to match her mommy's.

They all sat in bed eating off the same plate until
Kendall took a sip from her mug.

"We forgot my coffee, Daddy. My, my, my, what are
we going to do with you?"

The "my, my, my" belonged to Skylar Dawn's grandmother and was flawlessly reenacted. Her husband carefully moved from the bed so he wouldn't disturb the
tray of food. He bent at the waist and began backing
out of the bedroom.

"Your wish is my command."

Coffee for their daughter came as warm cocoa. It had to be in a mug that matched her parents'. Skylar Dawn reached across her and fiddled with the paper towel Kendall used as a napkin. She took her own and tucked it into exactly the same place on her pajamas.

"Do you want cotton jelly for the toast, sweetie?"

"Yes, please."

Kendall handed her the jelly-covered bread. The exchange went a little wonky, the toast flipping jelly-side down from Skylar Dawn's hands. It made a mess on the comforter they had draped over their laps.

"Oh furgle, furgle, furgle."

Kendall's heart stopped. *Jerry?* Her daughter was imitating a man she'd never met?

"Where did you hear that?" She turned to her daughter so fast it scared her.

"I'm sorry. I'm sorry." She began crying and grabbed Kendall's arm. "I know I wasn't supposed to tell anything."

"What's happened? She okay?" Heath asked, returning to the room and setting down the cocoa.

"I didn't mean to scare you, sweetie. I'm not mad." Kendall pushed the tray past her feet to the end of the bed.

"They said I couldn't ever tell or we'd get hurt. Bad hurt."

She held on to her daughter, wanting to forget everything. But she couldn't. *Those bastards.* "They can't hurt us, honey. I—I—I promise. Just tell me where you heard that word, okay?"

"I don't know. I think it was the house." Skylar Dawn sniffed.

"What house?" Heath asked.

"The one I didn't like. Please don't make me go back." She turned and buried her face in her daddy's chest, then pulled the covers over her head. "I'm sorry. I won't say it again. Promise."

"It's okay, baby. No one's making you go anywhere. You'll stay right here with us."

Heath looked over their hidden daughter's shape. Kendall moved her breakfast to the bedside table, then scooted close to her family. She and Heath soothed Skylar Dawn until she fell back to sleep. Heath tucked her in tight and nodded his head toward the doorway. Kendall joined him at the open door.

"I promised Skylar Dawn she wouldn't be alone." He lowered his deep voice. "Will you wake your mom up to sit with her while we talk about this?"

"I should check in and see if they've discovered anything." Her mind was spinning. *Jerry? How could that be?*

"Check in with who, Kendall? The only man we know who says *furgle*?"

"There has to be a different explanation. What if she heard it after he arrived? He's an FBI agent and used to be my partner. He can't be dirty."

"Agents can be bought just as easily as a store clerk. Who better to point your investigation in the wrong direction?"

She turned her face into his chest. "He knew every move we were making. Oh my God, Heath. Jerry kidnapped our baby. What are we going to do?"

"We're going to send that bastard to jail."

"How? Who's going to believe us?"

"We'll need a plan."

"Still, Heath. We have no real evidence. How can we

convince someone he's responsible because our daughter learned a new word?"

He pulled her into his arms, surrounding her in love and confidence.

"I know three men who won't hesitate to have faith."

Chapter Twenty-Four

With another long day ahead of them, Wade wished he had someone to call and talk to, like his fellow Rangers. Maybe it was because his three best friends each had a special someone now. He had watched Skylar Dawn go into her mother's arms and wanted…something. Anything.

"He's quitting," Slate announced as he walked through the office door.

"Who are you talking about?" Jack asked, right behind him.

"You mean Heath," Wade tried to confirm.

"Yes, I mean Heath. The guy I've been calling partner since I came to Company B."

"This is about you?" Jack said. "Not the fact that he almost lost his daughter and wife?"

"It's not for personal reasons." Slate sat on the corner of Jack's desk, looking at everyone around them. "Kendall has an offer in Portland, and he told her he'd quit the Rangers."

"How do you know this?" Major Clements asked, coming from his office.

"He said it to her after he knocked Marrone what's his-face on his back."

"Through his comm? That was private." Jack frowned.

"I can't help it if you guys didn't listen after they left the club and I did." Slate shrugged.

"You're not supposed to know this. He hasn't re-signed yet, Slate." Major Clements waved everyone back to work. "It ain't over until he actually does it."

"Yeah, he's going to. I know how much he wants to be with Kendall and Skylar Dawn. He's been moping around here for six months," Slate said.

"Hell, you're the one who's been complaining about how horrible he's been acting." Jack replied by pushing Slate off his desk.

"We have work to do, boys. We still need to find out what Public Exposure is up to. Why did they need Kendall out of the way? What had she discovered, and why did Bryan Marrone say a lot of people would be finding out what they were all about? Do we have a ticking clock?"

"As in a bomb or something?" Slate asked.

"We have no idea when, or if, this threat is actually going to occur." Jack began looking at his computer. "How are we going to narrow down what this event could be?"

"Right," Wade said.

"So we have access to Kendall's notes?" Major Clements paced between the desks.

"I don't, but I think we have something better now." He pointed at the door, and the couple who should have been at home.

"What the hell are they doing here?" their commander semi-yelled, but hugged Heath and Kendall as they entered. "We're glad you two have Skylar Dawn back safely. You guys should be home with her. We've got this covered."

"She's actually bouncing back pretty well. And she's in excellent hands. Josh and Tracey Parker brought their twins up to play." Heath wrapped his arm around Kendall's shoulders. She didn't pull away.

"Actually, Tracey brought the twins. Josh brought three Company F Rangers. They're at the house and not leaving until this is all behind us." Kendall laced her fingers with Heath's free hand.

Wade leaned back in his chair. The question on his mind was which Ranger called which Ranger. Josh offering to keep an eye on them was probably a safe bet. He probably didn't count on both Heath and Kendall coming back to the case.

"Why do you think we can't handle this without you? And why didn't you take this to the FBI since it's your case, Kendall?" Wade crossed his arms, waiting for the bomb.

"Because the FBI is in on it." Kendall dropped the words like an explosion.

"My office. Now," Major Clements commanded. "Slate, bring chairs for these two."

Wade grabbed the back of Heath's rolling chair, and Slate grabbed his own. They exchanged glances, and true to form, Slate smiled—most likely at the possibility of saving someone. He loved to be a hero.

In the major's office, Heath didn't hesitate to sit. The

beating he'd taken trying to protect his daughter had left him with two broken ribs and a hell of a lot of bruises.

Kendall waved off the chair and rubbed her bruising cheekbone. "I prefer to stand, thanks."

The last one inside the office, Jack closed the door. "Maybe you guys should start at the beginning."

"Agreed," Major Clements said.

"For months I've wondered how Public Exposure always seemed to be one step ahead of me. I could never get a break." Kendall paced, but kept her eyes on the major. "I was handed this case by my former partner. He'd been monitoring it, but kept saying nothing was there as the complaints grew. There was an immediate reluctance to give me resources or support."

The major sat on the corner of his desk. He'd known Kendall almost as long as they all had. He'd been at the wedding and at the hospital when Skylar Dawn was born. He'd cursed right along with all of them when she'd been kidnapped.

Wade didn't have to wonder if everyone believed Kendall. All they were waiting for was enough proof to act on it.

"I know now that Jerry Fisher, the supervisory special agent, asked to waive the conflict of interest regarding Heath helping the task force," the major said.

"He bet on us being at each other's throats and not making any progress," Heath said.

"Right. The thing is—" Kendall looked at him with admiration and love "—Heath's a damn good detective. We made headway that Jerry wasn't counting on. That's why he arranged to distract us by abducting Skylar Dawn."

"Distract?" Jack asked.

"Heath said from the beginning he thought the whole thing was a ruse to really get Kendall," Slate said.

"It was. Bryan Marrone stated he was instructed to keep me under wraps—"

"Or dead," Heath interrupted.

"—or dead," Kendall agreed.

"Other than his assignments, you haven't mentioned why you think Supervisory Special Agent Fisher is working with Public Exposure," the major pointed out.

"This is the part that's really thin." Heath wrapped his arm around his midsection and took a deep breath.

He and Kendall looked at each other. "Paper-thin," she agreed.

"Skylar Dawn has a habit of mimicking people she's around." Heath twisted in his seat to make eye contact with everyone. "For instance, she says 'my, my, my,' when imitating my mother-in-law. Or 'that's a relief,' which is something Kendall says."

"That's true. She even does my mom and dad after riding," Slate threw out.

"She hasn't been around Jerry since she was born. He's never been to the house. I've never taken her to work," said Kendall.

"And what's she saying now?" the major asked.

Kendall moved to stand behind Heath again. "Furgle."

"Paper-thin," Major Clements mumbled. Then he looked straight at the couple. "We can't march into the FBI headquarters and arrest a man because he says 'furgle'. What does that even mean?"

"I'll let you look that up, Major. It's an obscure word from *Catch-22*."

Heath stood. "Agreed, sir. But without him," he continued, "my family isn't going to be safe. I believe Marrone knows something, but I also think he'll never tell us. He talks about freaks being true believers. Yet he's bought into whatever they're selling."

"We know we're the only people who can get Special Agent Fisher to admit he was behind the kidnapping." Kendall moved to stand closer to the major. "He was one of three people who knew where Heath was on Friday. I remembered that early this morning. The other two are in this room. Slate wouldn't even tell *me*."

"In my defense, Heath asked me not to."

"I appreciate your loyalty. Even if it almost got my husband killed." Kendall laughed halfheartedly.

At least she could joke about it. Things could have gone in an entirely different direction if Slate hadn't called his mom to check on Heath and Skylar Dawn.

"Paper-thin," Major Clements said again. "If we get the warrant to search Special Agent Fisher's apartment for a device to read the flash drive…then and only then will we move forward."

"I suppose you two have already determined a plan of action?" Jack asked.

They both nodded. Kendall put her hands on Heath's shoulders. It was good to see them together. Really together.

"Kendall and I will go to his apartment and see if we can find the information," Heath began. "I could grab the devices, but then the encryption key might also be in the apartment—we'll have to make sure the warrant covers looking through items, etcetera."

"You don't need to do this. Any of us can plug in a flash drive," Slate said.

"When it comes to computers, I'm the best this Company B's got. You've all come to me for help. Sorry, but I'm not leaving it to one of you guys."

"Now all we need is the flash drive," Slate said. "There's no way Jerry will relinquish that into our custody," he added.

"I think I know a way." Kendall paused, and everyone looked in her direction. She looked only at Heath. "I didn't have a chance to tell you that the Public Exposure case has been moved to another agency. The agent in charge said she'd work with me if possible."

"Great. How do you contact her?"

"I'll need to contact Assistant Special Agent in Charge Steve Woods, and hopefully he'll tell Agent Ortis to contact me."

Agent Ortis? It couldn't be the same woman. The rest of the planning had lots of discussion and objections on both sides. Wade didn't hear much of it, until Slate punched him in the arm.

"What's up with you?" he asked behind a cupped hand. "Are you really going to let these two go after yesterday? That's a good idea?"

"Was I able to stop you or Jack from finishing what you started with your girlfriends? This is Heath's wife, his daughter. If he can walk, he's going to see it to the end."

Everyone looked at him. Yeah, everyone in the office had heard him.

"Damn straight," said Heath, Kendall and Jack while Major Clements nodded.

Wade leaned against the door, waiting. He opened it for Kendall when she stepped out to call Woods, and he stayed in the doorway of the break room while she dialed. She raised an eyebrow, silently asking if he wanted something. He did.

He couldn't think straight until he knew if this Agent Ortis was the Therese he'd been looking for since last year.

Kendall finished up with a smile on her face. "He's going to pass along the plan and see if they go for it. He wasn't surprised about Jerry. I wonder if they already knew."

"It might make the warrant easier if they did."

She pointed her finger toward the major's office. "Is there something else?"

"First...is Skylar Dawn okay? Do you guys need anything? I could watch the house after Company F leaves."

"We'll have to see, but thank you. Today, my mother promised to spend every minute with her. I think she's okay. Josh Parker's twins were kidnapped, and they took them to a counselor. They're calling a couple of people for a recommendation."

"That's good. That's good." He scratched his chin while Kendall looked at him strangely. "This might seem out of the blue but I was wondering...is the agent who took over the case *Therese* Ortis?"

"Yes, do you know her?"

"I believe we've met a couple of times."

"Small world, isn't it?" She scooted past him. "I should get back in there. Special Agent Woods said he'd have an answer pretty soon."

She turned around a few feet from him. "Would you

like me to tell her to give you a call? That is, if I see her. She seemed a little on the top secret side."

"No. No. That's okay. She knows how to find me."

Chapter Twenty-Five

Kendall entered Jerry's high-rise apartment building and issued the warrant to the supervisor. Heath entered covertly through the basement. They each took a different way to Jerry's apartment door. Major Clements was meeting with Steve Woods at the Dallas field office.

None of her coworkers had known the details of how they'd gotten Skylar Dawn back. They had to be right. It had to be Jerry. Therese hadn't reacted with surprise, and had been instrumental with the warrants coming through so quickly.

Everything inside Kendall told her Jerry worked for Public Exposure. It hadn't been easy, but they'd managed to get through most of the morning without tipping him off. Hopefully.

"We're keeping it quiet," Heath reminded her. "Remember, if he comes back before we're done, we wait for backup. No heroics. And no bashing the jerk's head in for what he did."

"Are you reminding me or you? Public Exposure can't know we've got him. I agreed to the plan, Heath. I'm fine with it. Even if I want to rip the man's head from his shoulders."

Once inside the apartment, the laptop was in plain sight. The password took a little longer to find. Heath pulled out desk drawers and looked on the bottom of small statues, pin holders, the stapler and tape dispenser until he found the current version inside a notebook.

"How did you—"

"A guess. He seems like the kind of guy who would use something complicated. But he doesn't seem like the type who can keep it in his head."

He began to access the information on Jerry's computer. She touched his shoulder before leaning in close to see what he found. With each screen, she was sure they were getting closer to arresting one of the men responsible for kidnapping their daughter.

"There it is," he said with an exaggerated sigh.

"That's a direct email from Brantley Lourdes. We've got him." She almost giggled in delight. "Are there any others?"

A noise in the hallway brought her back to earth super fast.

"Dammit. That's a key. Make the call."

Heath dialed his phone, connecting with Wade.

"What are you doing in here?" Jerry said as soon as the door swung wide. "I thought you were giving your statements. Why are you on my laptop?"

Kendall looked at her friend, her boss, her former partner. There wasn't any reason to pretend. Not any longer. "Why?"

"Why what?" Jerry asked innocently. But the recognition was there in his eyes. He knew they were on to him. "You have no right to be in my home."

Heath nodded in her direction, poised to plug in the flash drive. Hopefully the laptop would decrypt the file.

"Actually we have a warrant for your personal computer and cell phone, and to search your residence. Someone's at your office." She stuck out her left hand, leaving her right on her Glock. "I think I'll take your weapon while I'm at it."

"Slow down, Kendall. Are you going to arrest me? On what charge? You have no proof anything's been done," Jerry spouted as he looked back into the hallway.

Maybe. But at least with those words he sounded guilty.

Kendall flexed her fingers for him to hand over his weapon. "Heath and I already tossed a coin to see who took you down. Too bad for you that I won. Hand it over—now. Or I'll drop your face onto this expensive Italian tile."

Heath pulled his weapon.

"Okay. Okay." Jerry raised his hands.

"You messed up, Jerry," she told him. "While I was waiting on Heath to call me yesterday morning, you interrupted my phone call to Company B. You pointedly asked where I thought he was. You were the reason I stayed at the office instead of looking for him. And then you insisted on driving me to the ranch putting you at the scene so you could plant the phone."

"You're right, babe. But I think Jerry's smart enough to know that's all circumstantial. But wait," Heath nodded. "As hard as you might have tried, there was a fingerprint on the cell phone left on Stardust."

"Not yours, unfortunately," Kendall continued. "The kid who placed the SIM card inside and activated the bogus account? Turns out he's in the system and was oh too willing to pick you out of a photo lineup."

They might have been gloating. Just a little. But they had a right to be proud for doing their job. Both of them could have stayed home. They could have buried their heads under the covers and just been thankful they were all alive.

That wasn't what men like Heath did. Because he was a better man, he made her a better person, too.

"I really don't understand how you got into bed with that vile piece of slime. You stole my daughter, Jerry." She advanced a step, really wanting to plant his face in the floor. "Hand over your gun or I'll consider it resisting."

"Don't do anything stupid, Kendall." Jerry splayed his hands. He drew back his jacket and took his service weapon from its holster with two fingers. "There's definitely been a mistake."

"We know you were one of the kidnappers."

"Skylar Dawn mimicked your idiotic use of *furgle*," Heath threw out. "Got it. I'll have files open any minute. The file might take longer."

"Okay, okay. I was hired by Brantley Lourdes. You should be thanking me for saving her. They wanted you both to disappear. At least I put the kid someplace safe."

"She was safe with me." Heath stepped from around the desk.

"We've got him, Heath. All of them."

"I don't think you know exactly who or what you're up against. This won't end with you taking me to the Bureau. Public Exposure is bigger than Brantley Lourdes."

"Save it for later." She took handcuffs from her jacket

pocket. "We'll nail Brantley Lourdes *and* Public Exposure. You should start worrying about the deal you're going to broker."

He turned around, but only one hand came behind his back. Before she could say furgle, he'd reached out and grabbed a hidden snub nose revolver. He spun again, aiming it at her head.

"Drop it, Heath. Or I swear I will shoot out her control center and your kid will have a vegetable for a mom if she's not six feet under."

Heath dropped his gun on the desk.

"Now, pull the flash drive and join your wife." He directed them toward the open door. "Uh-uh. Keep those hands up."

Their backup would be there any minute. But Heath's phone that was relaying all the information to them was still on the desk. Moving as slowly as possible, they made it to the elevator.

"How could you have betrayed us? Betrayed your country?"

"There you go getting all dramatic again, Kendall. Money, and knowing where the nonextradition countries are." Jerry laughed. "Basically lots of money."

Heath looked from Jerry to her and reluctantly backed onto the elevator when the doors opened. Standing closest to the panel, Jerry pushed a button, and then pulled a second gun strapped around his ankle to point directly at Heath's chest.

"No." She moved between Heath and the barrel. Jerry might be reluctant to shoot her, but not her husband.

The elevator began its descent. Heath's hands were

on her shoulders, trying to push her to the side. She stood firm.

This was her fault. She hadn't cuffed him soon enough. Could he get to the second Beretta under her jacket she'd put there for just this reason? She crossed her arms to disguise any movement he might make.

"Don't try it. Keep your hands up exactly where I can see them, Heath. Turn around and put your hands on his shoulders, Kendall." Jerry held his gun steady.

She turned her back to the traitor and held Heath's steady gaze. The pressure in his hands exuded trust and confidence. Jerry pulled her gun and his cell, then stuck his snub nose into her back. She continued to look into her love's eyes.

"What are you going to do when we get to the ground floor?" She meant it for Heath, not Jerry. She'd need his help to take this bastard down before he shot both of them.

Heath frowned and pressed four fingers into her right shoulder, then three, then two… He'd understood her question. She needed to know what floor they were on if they were to do this together.

"You are the only *one* for me, babe," she said to let him know when they should act. Now they just had to survive the ten-floor descent.

"Believe it or not, Kendall, you've brought this on yourself by being too damn good at your job," Jerry said. "If you had just walked away. I gave you a lot of opportunities to shut the file on this thing."

Heath's fingers pressed into her shoulder, counting down the floors. It was risky, but the close quarters could work to her advantage. They had to act before they reached the basement.

"I'm afraid I'm going to have to get rid of you both."

The basement floor indicator dinged.

The doors began to open. She let the rage, terror and love all mix together to create a surge of energy. She leaned forward against Heath and kicked backward, hitting Jerry's chest. Heath shoved her aside, and she hit the wall as he rammed the traitor in the chest. The momentum carried the men down, and they fell to the hard elevator floor, between the doors, keeping them from closing.

The gun blast made her ears ring. Heath pounded Jerry's wrist against the floor until the gun skidded down the slick garage floor. Heath kept Jerry down with his weight. She added his strength to hers, but soon pulled back, taking Heath with her.

Jerry didn't move. He was out cold. Heath pulled them away from the traitor. He checked for a pulse, then rolled Jerry to his stomach, pulling Jerry's arms behind him and resting his knee and body weight there.

He stretched out a hand and pulled her close for a hard quick kiss, then his hands were searching her arms. "You okay? You weren't hit or anything, were you?"

"I'm fine. His shot didn't get you?"

"No, I'm good." He gave her another quick kiss.

"You really are." She pulled her badge and pointed to her Glock as the second elevator doors opened, and a security guard ran toward them. "Special Agent Kendall Barlow. He's a Texas Ranger. Could you direct our backup down here? We're taking this man into custody."

The guard didn't move, but the second set of elevator doors opened again and Heath's team was there for the save.

"Took you guys long enough."

"Did you find the elevators kind of slow here?" Slate said.

"Did you get all that on tape?"

"Right up until you left the apartment."

Heath put an arm around her, pulling her farther away. "First off, I regret not getting to hit you for what you did to my wife and daughter. And basically the hell you've put me through. Keep that in mind before I get on that elevator to escort you upstairs."

"Heath," everyone cautioned.

"You've got one chance, man. Where is Public Exposure attacking this afternoon, and where is Brantley Lourdes?" He lowered his voice so that only Kendall and Jerry could hear. "One shot to answer, or you're mine. Alone with me for as many floors as this building has, and then back down."

Chapter Twenty-Six

Heath let the Rangers talk around him and over him in the apartment garage while he sat in Wade's truck. He was actually too tired to think about anything. He didn't know whose back seat he occupied. He just needed to close the windows and not move for a month.

He was too exhausted and in too much pain. He'd been holding it together on aspirin and having his ribs bound with an ACE bandage. But damn, he and Kendall looked as bad as they felt for once.

"Here, take these." Kendall dropped two extra-strength somethings in his palm and handed him a bottle of water. "It's all I could find. I think you could still take a painkiller the doctor prescribed when you get to the house. Wade and Slate both volunteered to take you home."

Bruised and broken physically, but not down and out. They'd won. They had Skylar Dawn. They had the man who had orchestrated her kidnapping. So why didn't he feel that it was over?

"What's wrong with my truck?" He pushed himself to a sitting position, waiting for her to explain. Images of someone swiping it raced through his head.

"We're in no shape to drive, remember?"

"I'll wait around until you finish. We should both see Skylar Dawn together."

"That's just it—"

"One down, one to go." Slate swooshed his hands together like he was dusting off. "The threat of being alone in the elevator with Heath really scared the pants off your boss. He talked a little, but lawyered up."

"I'm sure all the Rangers standing behind Heath helped convince Jerry to disclose where Brantley Lourdes was staying."

"What do you mean, 'one down, one to go'? Are they arresting Brantley Lourdes?" Heath looked at Slate for the answer.

"You ready to go, or should I let you guys talk?" Wade pointed toward his truck. The one Heath was currently using.

"Were you trying to get me out of here before you took off to follow another lead?" Heath turned to Kendall. "Are you trying to question him without me?"

"Actually, you're both heading home," Major Clements informed him. "You have only two options—the hospital or the comfort of your own bed. Which is it going to be?"

Heath slid across the seat, attempting to hide the winces and groans.

"Give up, Lieutenant. You can barely stand. You won't be any good out there if you pass out. Time to go home to your little girl," the Major said.

"He's right." Kendall extended a hand to help him from the truck.

He had to admit defeat by sitting on the edge of the

seat. "What about you? Somehow I'm getting the impression that you have different plans." He wouldn't let her go without him. "At this moment, Lourdes is still out there and you're at risk."

"I'd be fine, but I told them I need to head home. They're sending the new agent who's in charge of the case here. She has a couple of questions."

"Why didn't you say so?" He tried to push himself to stand on his own.

"We've had a couple of interruptions," she whispered.

Most of the time he was a tough guy. Now...not so much. Wade and Slate each claimed a side, ready to help. Wade's fingers began clenching his biceps as a dark-haired woman walked into their circle.

"Kendall. Heath...if I may? I'm Special Agent Therese Ortis." She stepped forward to shake his hand. "I have a few questions for you both. Then you can head home. I'd be glad to catch you next week for your full statement."

That look. The shy moment when two people who know each other try to keep it a secret. It happened between Therese and Wade. Heath had a hunch, but he'd respect their bare acknowledgment of each other.

"What can we do for you, Agent Ortis?"

"I'd like to face Brantley Lourdes with a little more knowledge of his group. Why did you think the word *furgle* was so unusual?"

"Jerry used it on Kendall more than once when he was her partner." Heath's dislike of the man had begun as soon as they'd looked up the meaning.

"It's a word used in the book *Catch-22*. Jerry always used it out of context, and I didn't appreciate it," Kendall said.

"We found the book upstairs in his bookshelves. But you never reported him for his actions?"

"She told me, but she took care of the problem herself," Heath answered.

"Did Special Agent Fisher read a lot?"

"Not really," Kendall said.

"Would it surprise you to know we found at least thirty top literary titles?"

"Yes. He doesn't talk about reading. I'm not certain what that means, though." She thought of something important. Her mouth formed a perfect O before she pulled out her phone. "Heath, what's your password to your backup file for your phone? You know, the one where your photos are stored automatically."

"The same as it's always been." *K-n-H-4ever.* He still believed that could happen. "What did you remember?"

"The pictures you took of Saundra Rosa's crime scene. There's one." She rapidly swiped through the pictures. "There's the other."

She flipped the phone toward Agent Ortis.

"They have the same books. This is great. The books are their key. I can work with this. Good work. I'll be in touch."

"Let's get out of here." He lifted his arm and waited for Kendall to dip her shoulder under it to hold him steady while they walked to his truck.

Once out of the apartment garage, they continued around the block to where he'd parked and his partners were waiting to drive them home.

"You made the agency come to you," he said once

they reached the truck. "I didn't think you'd ever walk away from a case."

"One thing I think we've both realized this week is how important our family is. We're needed at home."

He handed her the keys and she helped him into the passenger seat.

"Did you see the way Wade looked at Therese Ortis?" Kendall sounded lighthearted and teasing by the time she had her door shut. "I swear, I think he's got a thing for her."

"She has to be the informant who saved his life after that beating he took. Before we left, Jack told her that Megan would be in town this weekend." He could play along and avoid the all-important question of which room he'd be sleeping in tonight.

"Oh my gosh, so much has happened that I forgot to tell you Jack is supposed to propose. I guess those plans are on hold."

"Good for him. He's been head over heels for Megan since they met."

"What about Slate and his new love life?" Kendall turned onto the highway, heading home.

"Vivian wants to get back on her feet, but they're still exclusive. Is that the word nowadays? I've been away from that rodeo for a while now and was never that much into it before I met you."

"Really? Come to think of it, you've never mentioned any old girlfriends. Surely you had a girl in every city." His wife smiled. Teased. Winked and smiled some more.

He shook his head, afraid to break the relaxed atmosphere inside the truck's cab.

"Not even in college?" she asked.

"I think I told you things got hard about that time. I worked at the ranch in Alpine every spare minute I had. Mom needed my help so I lived at home."

"Unlike my mother, who has never needed help. Sometimes I wonder…"

"Wonder what?"

Kendall stopped at the corner of their street. "I wonder if she did…you know, if she needed someone, she might actually find a person who makes her happy."

THERE WERE FOUR Rangers guarding her house and visitors inside. Kendall hesitated to drive the truck into the driveway, wondering how to tell Heath she needed a little time. He reached over and took her hand. Maybe he'd sensed her hesitation. Maybe she needed some type of explanation for how well he knew her.

"I need time to figure this out. Alone. My emotions are all mixed up."

"Take all the time you need. Moving is a big decision for all of us."

"I'm just an emotional wreck right now," she finished with a long involuntary sigh, shutting the engine off in their driveway.

"I get it." He caught her hand, bringing it to his lips and making her smile. "Wait. Before we go inside, I've been trying to say this all week. So bear with me."

"I just need a little time—"

"Sweetheart. It's my turn. I'm going to respect your time, but I think I need to move back in for a while. I love you and Skylar Dawn more than life. I thought my biggest fear was if something happened to the two of you because of work."

"But it was my job."

"Just hear me out." He scratched his chin. "I found out that's not my biggest fear. That would be living without you."

"And Skylar Dawn."

The squeals of children at play inside the house brought her statement home.

"Honestly, she'll always be my daughter. Nothing will be able to take that away. No matter how far away she is or whether or not I live in the same house. I don't want to grow old without you. And believe me, I'm feeling the creaking bones earlier than I thought I would." He rubbed his ribs with his free hand. "You don't have to say anything now. I'm sorry for all the assumptions and for leaving you alone. I should have just told you that a long time ago."

Her hand shook. "For one of those strong, silent cowboy types…you know just what to say."

They got out of the truck. He stood on his own, not needing her help. She liked helping him, enjoyed him leaning on her—literally. It was a reason to touch him and feel safe.

More sounds of children playing had her feet moving up the steps. She waited at the top for him.

"I'm going to talk to the guys before I head inside. But—" His brow crinkled in concentration.

"What?"

He stepped up and pulled her into his arms, kissing her like it was the first time. Exploring her mouth, accepting her passionate response.

"I love you, Kendall. I always will."

He waited as she turned and quietly opened the door and then clicked it closed. No one heard her come inside. She let him go without telling him. She leaned against the door with her hand on the knob about to return to him.

"Real pretty speech." Bryce, the Ranger who had stayed at the corner of the porch, had hung back until she'd come inside. "She'll come around."

She waited. There was a long pause before Heath responded. "I don't know. There's been a lot of space between us in the past six months."

"I have the first shift on your porch tonight before your partner takes over. He's ready to take you to the ranch. If that's really where you want to go."

"Need. Not want."

"Like I said, she'll come around before you know it. See you in the morning."

She ran down the hallway away from the door, away from Heath.

Did she really need to think about their situation? She was emotional and out of control. Waiting was the logical thing to do. And she'd always been logical. Waiting to make a choice—that was the way to go.

So why was her heart breaking again without him by her side?

Chapter Twenty-Seven

Why had he come to the rodeo? He'd gotten up early to feed the horses after a restless night of tossing in his bed alone. But he'd needed to get away from the ranch. Needed to get away from everyone really. Needed to be with people who weren't worried about him.

His parents' house was too far away to visit and be back to work in a couple of days—if he could concentrate on anything. It had been less than a full day. He couldn't go by himself, and he didn't want Kendall to think he was pressuring her for an answer. Instead, he reassured his mom that he was okay via text...about every three hours.

Hell, maybe he *should* pack up Jupitar and take a trip home to see his mom and dad. The major had looked him in the eye and told him he'd put him on desk duty for six months if he showed up for work sooner than a week.

But the major didn't know Heath was sleeping on the couch. Officially...he didn't have a home at the moment. Maybe that was the real reason he'd come to help at the rodeo. He didn't want everyone to know he wasn't with Skylar Dawn and Kendall.

Dammit, he was a chicken after all. Even his morning ride had lost its appeal.

"What are you out here for, Heath? Did that bronc throw you a little softer than we thought last week?" the manager of the rodeo asked.

"Afraid I've got some broken ribs, Bobby Joe."

"And you're spending your free time here? Don't you have a life, kid?" He cupped Heath's shoulder before he walked off to the next thing he had to do.

A rhetorical question that shot straight through his heart. He didn't want to think. His thoughts would only land on Kendall. And who knew how long she'd take. He might not know what to say or when the right time to say it was…but she always needed time to think.

And he always gave it to her.

"So what do you say, cowboy? What are you doing after you're finished?" asked a sweet voice he recognized but didn't expect to hear.

Heath dropped the edge of his Stetson to block the sun from his eyes. "Kendall?"

"I had to come down here to make sure the rodeo groupies were behaving themselves." She wore her tightest, lowest-cut jeans and had her shirt tied in a knot just under her breasts.

"I'd let out a howl but it might draw attention to you."

"And that's bad?"

"Sure it is. No way do I want to share your company."

"Oh. Really?" She turned to face him.

"You can't be surprised."

"I'm just… I'm not very good at flirting anymore."

He looked around, searching for their daughter. She was with the Parkers, heading for the stands. Two ad-

ditional Rangers from Company F flanked her and his
mother-in-law. Bryce hung back, waiting on Kendall.

Her shy mannerisms reminded him of his ability to
get tongue-tied. He tried not to crowd her when cowboys passed by and needed more space. But he liked
crowding in close to her.

"I see Skylar Dawn found her hat," he said, tipping
his up a little to see her better.

"Actually, Josh's twins asked to visit Stardust. You
know they have their own horses. I agreed because I
thought you went to the ranch." She stuck her fingers
into the front pockets of her jeans, but they didn't disappear very far because they were super tight.

It had been awhile since he'd seen her in his world.
Jeans and boots looked great on her. The wolf whistles
would start pretty soon if he didn't get her shirt untied
from under her breasts and tucked into her waistband.

"Anyway, we went out there this morning. We might
have to get her a bunch of farm animals after what the
Parkers were telling her about baby pigs and chickens."

"We?"

"Dammit. I'm going to sound crazy, but I don't need
time to think about whether I love you or not." She
threw her arms around his neck.

"You sure? You seemed to have a plan to wait yesterday. Waiting is sort of your thing."

"That's ridiculous. If I knew what I was doing, don't
you think I'd be doing it right now? I'm stumbling
around in the dark."

She switched her hands into her back pockets, drawing even more stares from the cowboys.

"Hey, babe. It's kind of chilly out here. Do you have

a sweater?" Heath didn't wait for an answer, he took his jean jacket off and draped it over her shoulders.

THE MEN BEHIND them laughed. Kendall waved, flirting a little more by dropping the jacket off one shoulder. The wolf whistles ensued. Bryce covered his laugh behind his hand. Heath glared then looked up toward their daughter to smile.

"Changing the subject, Skylar Dawn seems to be doing okay. She's walking around without you and laughing." He waved at the stands.

"Jackson and Sage have talked a little about how scary it was to be kidnapped. They've been a big help. Our daughter is bouncing back faster than I thought possible." She turned to wave at everyone in the stands.

"Enjoy the show, Bryce. I can take care of my wife for a while," he said in a louder voice. "Maybe we should go somewhere we can talk?"

"Home?" she asked.

"I was thinking about a walk around the pens. That is, if you don't mind the smell." Heath wrapped his arm around her waist and guided her behind the staging area.

Kendall tugged his arm to head to a secluded corner. "What do you say, Heath? Will you give me another chance to get this right?"

"I don't want to go through life without you, sweetheart. I love you."

"I love you, too. And I'm *asking* you to help me decide about our future."

Heath took off his hat, circled it in the air and let out a big cowboy holler. He grabbed his ribs and winced, but not for long before he pulled her into his arms and kissed her.

When he let her up for air she told him, "I'm ready to ride off into the sunset, cowboy."

* * * * *

Look for the next book in USA TODAY
bestselling author Angi Morgan's
TEXAS BROTHERS OF COMPANY B *miniseries,*
RANGER WARRIOR, available next month.

And don't miss the previous titles in the
TEXAS BROTHERS OF COMPANY B *series:*

RANGER PROTECTOR
RANGER DEFENDER

Available now from Harlequin Intrigue!

I N T R I G U E

Available July 17, 2018

#1797 COWBOY ABOVE THE LAW
The Lawmen of McCall Canyon • by Delores Fossen
When Deputy Court McCall's father is shot, Court's top suspect is
Rayna Travers, his former lover. And yet, her injuries force her to seek protection
in Court's arms. But can he trust her claims of innocence without falling for her
again?

#1798 THREE COURAGEOUS WORDS
Mission: Six • by Elle James
The last person navy SEAL "Buck" Graham Buckner expects to see in Sudan is
his first love, Dr. Angela Vega. She's there helping those who can't afford health
care, and his mission is to keep her from falling into the clutches of the warlord
Buck has been sent to stop.

#1799 AVALANCHE OF TROUBLE
Eagle Mountain Murder Mystery • by Cindi Myers
A double murder and a missing child bring Deputy Gage Walker and
Maya Renfro, the sister of one of the victims, together. They become partners
on and off the case as they search for Maya's missing neice. The orphan may
not be as far away as they think...

#1800 ARMED RESPONSE
Omega Sector: Under Siege • by Janie Crouch
Someone is making SWAT team member Lillian Muir look like she's helping
a terrorist, and former Special Forces soldier Jace Eakins is brought in to
investigate. Will the former lovers be able to put aside their shared history?
Or will their secrets consume them, leaving the terrorist at large?

#1801 COWBOY'S SECRET SON
by Robin Perini
When Courtney Jamison walks back into Jared King's life, she brings a
surprise—Jared has a son. And she and the boy have become a killer's target.
Haunted by his past, will Jared be able to save the baby he never knew about...
and the woman he never forgot?

#1802 THE DEPUTY'S BABY
The Protectors of Riker County • by Tyler Anne Snell
Seven months after a one-night stand, dispatcher Cassie Gates learns that
Henry Ward, the father of her unborn child, has been hired as her department's
new deputy. As Cassie and Henry rediscover each other, a mysterious man
warns that the county faces impending doom.

Get 4 FREE REWARDS!

We'll send you 2 FREE Books
plus 2 FREE Mystery Gifts.

Harlequin® Intrigue books feature heroes and heroines that confront and survive danger while finding themselves irresistibly drawn to one another.

FREE Value Over **$20**

She couldn't see the bastard behind her but knew he was waiting. Waiting to watch her die as her strength gave out and she couldn't support herself anymore.

She tried to yell—even if someone came rushing into the room, it wasn't going to do much more damage than her swaying here until her strength gave out—but the sound was cut off by the rope over her vocal cords. If she wanted to yell, she was going to have to use one hand to pull the rope away from the front of her throat. That meant supporting all her weight with one arm.

Her muscles were already straining from the constant state of pulling up. Supporting her weight with one arm wasn't going to work.

But she'd be damned if she was just going to die in front of this bastard.

She swung her legs up, trying to catch the upper part of the rope, but failed again. Even if she could get her legs hooked up there, she wasn't going to be able to get herself released.

She heard a low chuckle to her side. Bastard. He was enjoying this.

And then the alarm started blaring.

Masked Man muttered a curse and took off up the stairs. Lillian felt her arms begin to shake as the exhaustion from holding her own weight began to take its toll. If it wasn't for the rigorous SWAT training, she'd already be dead.

But even training wouldn't be enough. Physics would win. Her arms began to tremble more and she was forced to let go of the rope to give them a break.

Immediately the rope cut off all oxygen.

When everything began to go black, she reached up and grabbed the rope again. It wasn't long before the tremors took over.

She didn't want to go out like this. Wished she hadn't squandered this second chance she'd had with Jace in her life.

But even thinking of Jace, with his gorgeous blue eyes and cocky grin that still did things to her heart after all these years, couldn't give her any more strength.

She reached back up with her arms and found them collapsing before she even took her weight. Then the noose tightened and jerked around her neck, pulling her body forward, all air gone.

Blackness.

Will Jace and the team get there in time to rescue her? Find out when USA TODAY *bestselling author Janie Crouch's* ARMED RESPONSE *goes on sale August 2018.*
Look for it wherever Harlequin® Intrigue books are sold!

www.Harlequin.com

SPECIAL EXCERPT FROM

*An engagement of convenience might be the only thing
that can save his family's ranch, but Lucian Granger's
sudden attraction to his bride-to-be, Karlee O'Malley,
will change everything he thought he knew about love…*

*Enjoy a sneak peek at THE LAST RODEO,
part of the A WRANGLER'S CREEK NOVEL series
by USA TODAY bestselling author Delores Fossen.*

Karlee walked out onto the ground of the barn where
Lucian had busted his butt eighteen times while competing
in the rodeo. Perhaps he saw this party as a metaphorical
toss from a bronc, but if so, there was no trace of that in his
expression. He smiled, his gaze sliding over her, making
her thankful she'd opted for a curve-hugging dress and the
shoes.

Lucian walked toward her, and the moment he reached
her, he curved his arm around her waist, pulled her to him.

And he kissed her.

The world dissolved. That included the ground beneath
her feet and every bone in her body. This wasn't like the
other stiff kiss in his office. Heck, this wasn't like any other
kiss that'd happened—ever.

The feel of him raced through Karlee, and what damage
the lip-lock didn't do, his scent finished off. Leather and
cowboy. A heady mix when paired with his mouth that she
was certain could be classified as one of the deadly sins.

She heard the crowd erupt into pockets of cheers, but
all of that noise faded. The only thing was the soft sound

of pleasure she made. Lucian made a sound, too. A manly grunt. It went well with that manly grip he had on her and his manly taste. Jameson whiskey and sex. Of course, that sex taste might be speculation on her part since the kiss immediately gave her many, many sexual thoughts.

Lucian eased back from her. "You did good," he whispered.

That dashed the sex thoughts. It dashed a lot of things because it was a reminder that this was all for show. But Lucian didn't move away from her after saying that. He just stood there, looking down at her with those scorcher blue eyes.

"You did good, too," Karlee told him because she didn't know what else to say.

He still didn't back away despite the fact the applause and cheers had died down and the crowd was clearly waiting for something else to happen. Karlee was waiting, as well. Then it happened.

Lucian kissed her again.

This time, though, it wasn't that intense smooch. He just brushed his mouth over hers. Barely a touch but somehow making it the most memorable kiss in the history of kisses. Ditto for the long, lingering look he gave her afterward.

"That was from me," he said, as if that clarified things. It didn't. It left Karlee feeling even more aroused. And confused.

What the heck did that mean?

Will this pretend engagement lead to happily-ever-after?

Find out in THE LAST RODEO
by USA TODAY *bestselling author Delores Fossen,*
available now.

www.Harlequin.com